D1459014

LANCASHIRE COUNTY LIBRARY

3011813577484 6

Gunfight at Copper Creek

Texas, 1874: when ex-cavalrymen Ben Turner and Wes Noble arrive in Copper Creek, they discover the town is being held to ransom by a gang of gunslingers, led by ruthless local rancher Ed Holden, and that the law in the town is non-existent; its most recent marshal left town rather than face Holden's men. Nevertheless, Turner and Noble opt to settle in Copper Creek and buy the town's general store, only to find themselves subject to demands for payment for the 'protection' that Holden insists on from the town's merchants. Turner and Noble, however, have other ideas. . . .

By the same author

Buffalo Falls

Gunfight at Copper Creek

Robert B. McNeill

A Black Horse Western

ROBERT HALE

© Robert B. McNeill 2017
First published in Great Britain 2017

ISBN 978-0-7198-2250-6

The Crowood Press
The Stable Block
Crowood Lane
Ramsbury
Marlborough
Wiltshire SN8 2HR

www.bhwesterns.com

Robert Hale is an imprint
of The Crowood Press

The right of Robert B. McNeill to be identified as
author of this work has been asserted by him
in accordance with the Copyright, Designs and
Patents Act 1988

LANCASHIRE COUNTY LIBRARY	
3011813577484 6	
Askews & Holts	19-Jun-2017
AF WES	£14.50
STA	

CPI Group (UK) Ltd, Croydon, CR0 4YY

CHAPTER ONE

The Mescalero Apaches had trailed us for better than thirty minutes. We first sighted them on a ridge to our left an hour after we left Las Cruces and began riding into the Mesilla Valley. The party appeared to be around sixteen in number, among them a rider on a burro who kept lagging behind.

Ben Turner and I had stopped at Las Cruces to resupply. We'd panned the Canadian River for four months and had us a gunny sack of ore worth $800. Mostly it was flour gold, though there were some small nuggets in the mix.

When we discovered that the trader in Las Cruces paid only five dollars an ounce we sold him just eight ounces to buy what was needed. The El Paso assayer paid double that, which was why we were headed there.

A light breeze picked up a nearby tumbleweed and Ben reined his bay clear.

'Don't look like a hunting party to me, Wes,' he said, nodding towards the ridge. 'The rider on the burro don't look Apache, neither.'

I had a pair of Bullock's binoculars in my saddle-bag. I took them out, trained them on the ridge, and thumbed the centre wheel till I got focus.

'There's a little fat fella on the burro, looks American,' I said. 'The Indians on either side are harrying him to keep up. They're decked out in warpaint.'

No sooner had I spoken than the Indian in front raised a shout and the horde rode down the slope towards us, leaving only two riders flanking the American. The valley where we were at that point was flat, and the only cover was a grove of piñon trees fifty yards ahead. The Apaches urged their ponies on, quickly shortening the distance between us.

'Think we can outrun 'em, Ben?' I asked.

'No, I don't,' he replied. 'The Apache ponies are carrying less weight. Head for those trees. It'll give us some cover.'

We rode hell for leather to the piñon grove, where we dismounted and hurriedly tethered our mounts. Ben drew his Spencer from the saddle

6

scabbard and I took my Henry. The group was almost upon us when we sighted our rifles and began firing. The Indians took their usual attack approach of encircling and shooting from their ponies, each brave hunkering low to make himself less of a target.

We were significantly outnumbered. I counted thirteen Indians, all armed with Winchester repeaters. The saving grace was that none of them had a particularly good aim. A bullet stripped the bark from a branch near my ear, but otherwise no shot came close. But neither Ben nor I had been able to find our marks either. Things changed a little when one of Ben's rounds caught a young Indian in the shoulder; he fell from his horse and bounced along the ground for a moment, then lay still.

'If they get any nearer there's a chance of them rushing us,' I said.

'I'd say that's their plan,' Ben replied. 'They've started to draw in their noose. I've seen it before, with Arapahos in Wyoming before the war. We came to the rescue of a group of settlers who'd circled their wagons. The Indians kept firing, all the while getting closer. They rushed in and finally overcame the pioneers.'

I fired as we spoke and my round ricocheted off

the base plate of an Apache rifle. It hit the head of a pony behind, causing the the animal to fall and throw its rider. The Indian somersaulted, appeared to hang in the air, then landed on his stomach. The fall knocked the wind out of him and his face kissed the dirt. Ben and I stood back to back then, in an attempt to fight off the attack at either side.

But the Indians were now only an arm's length away.

'They're getting ready to dismount,' Ben said, then he put down his rifle and drew his Army Colt. 'We're gonna have us a close-quarters fight.'

Ben shot at the first Indian to dismount, but almost at once five more leapt from their ponies and hit the ground running. They rushed in and grappled Ben just as the trigger was pulled. The bullet flew wide, and the Apache targeted quickly joined the others and wrestled Ben to the ground. He fought back, landing a blow with his pistol to the head one of them before being overpowered.

While this was happening I got off a final shot. The round tore the rifle from the hands of the Indian I'd aimed at: the one who'd made war-whoops when he and his braves first charged us.

The moment the Henry discharged I felt a kick in my back. I hit the ground and the remaining Apaches fell on me and held me down. They bound my wrists in front with rope, then hauled me back to my feet. I looked over and saw Ben was now also standing, held by two Indians. Like me, his hands were tied at the wrists.

A minute or so later the Apaches untethered our horses and their leader gestured us to remount. The brave whose shoulder had been creased and the one who was winded both appeared to have recovered. They approached Ben and me and the older one made threatening gestures. The leader spoke to them sharply in Apache; they turned away sulkily and fell in at the back, the older one doubling up on the younger man's pony.

As Ben and I struggled to mount, the Indians who'd stayed behind rode up, still flanking the man on the burro. The leader beckoned to the taller of the two and they spoke for a minute. The brave walked his pony over to us.

'My name is Grey Owl,' he said. He nodded to the leader, then looked at me. 'He is called Lone Wolf. He say you good rifleman; you aim well to shoot Winchester from his hands.' Grey Owl pointed to the man on the burro.

'He also tell me to tell you this man is being taken to our camp for trial. Yesterday, four white men kill children and squaws while Apache men on antelope hunt. We search for them. Now we take you to our camp also. If woman who survive say any of you with the men who do this thing, we kill you and take scalp.'

The man on the burro was around forty and wore a woollen suit and a derby hat. He took a kerchief from his pocket and mopped sweat from his face.

'Those killings got nothing to do with me, fellas,' he said. 'I've been trying to tell them but they won't listen. My name's Grover Bannister. I'm a drummer with a tailoring supplier in Silver City. Set out for El Paso from Las Cruces early this morning. Hadn't covered but five miles before this bunch attacked. They shot my horse from under me. Cut my sample bags from my burro and made me ride it.'

Grey Owl swung his pony around, went over to Bannister and cuffed him on the cheek.

'I told you before – no talk,' he said, then he turned to us and placed a finger to his mouth. 'We ride now. No more talk.'

We rode for an hour until we came to two bluffs called Twin Buttes. The Apaches took a left fork off the main trail there and followed it till they came to an area wooded with tall pines, where they took a narrow path to the right. This wound for several miles through the trees until it reached a fast-flowing river. Here it narrowed even further, and after another mile we came to a clearing where the

10

Apaches had their camp.

The Indians who watched our approach were mainly squaws and children, but as we rode further into the village we saw a number of young adolescent males, who stared at us with undisguised hostility.

The encampment comprised forty or more tepees. Our captors led us to an open space in the middle where there was a large campfire. Lone Wolf dismounted and walked to a tepee more lavishly decorated than the others. He went inside; a minute later he reappeared with an older Indian who wore a cloth headband from which two feathers protruded.

'The chief?' I whispered to Ben.

'Yeah, I'd say so,' he replied.

Lone Wolf said something to the others and they dismounted and gestured for Bannister, Ben and me to do likewise. The Indians then held each of us by the arms and took us to where Lone Wolf and the older Apache stood. The Indian who, we guessed, was the chief then beckoned to Grey Owl, who went over to the older Apache and spoke to him.

When the chief had finished speaking Grey Owl nodded, then took a knife from his waistband and began walking towards us.

Bannister began to shake and we realized that he anticipated the worst.

'Please, don't kill me,' he said. 'I wasn't involved in any murders. Believe me, I'm innocent.'

CHAPTER TWO

Grey Owl reached out and cut the ropes from Bannister's wrists, then freed Ben and me.

'White Bear, our chief, say while here you our guests, not be tied,' he said. 'We eat now, you share. Woman who see the killers join us after meal. She look at you, to see if she ...' He paused and looked at us quizzically. 'Don't remember American word. Mean *to know face*.'

'Recognize,' Ben told him.

'That's the word,' Grey Owl nodded. 'To see if she recognize any of you. If she say you not these men, we let you go,'

'That's OK. Wes and I aren't the men you're looking for,' Ben said. 'We're prospectors on our way to El Paso to sell a little gold.'

Grey Owl nodded again and indicated the fire.

'Sit,' he said.

Ben and I and Bannister went to the hearth and sat. We were joined by Lone Wolf and Grey Owl, together with White Bear and two other tribal elders. More logs were heaped on the fire and strips of antelope meat were roasted and given to us. We ate, and between mouthfuls White Bear and the others became engaged in animated conversation.

Bannister still looked worried.

'Do you really think they mean to let us go if the woman says we weren't involved?' he whispered.

'Most likely,' Ben replied. 'They generally honour their word.'

'I'm surprised they have a camp here,' Bannister said. 'I thought the Apaches had been given land in Arizona. Cochise signed a treaty last year.'

'It was two years ago, 1872,' Ben replied. 'But several of the Mescalero tribes were allowed to remain. For the time being, anyway.'

'What if the woman blames us, says she can't tell the difference between white men?' Bannister said.

Ben eyed Bannister's portly frame and a smile played around the corners of his mouth.

'Oh, I don't think you need worry. We don't look that much alike.'

As we were talking a middle-aged squaw made her way into the clearing and stood near White

Bear's tent. She looked at the three of us intently for a moment and stood quietly.

'I think we'll soon know,' I said, nodding in her direction. 'I'd say that woman's their witness.'

White Bear finished eating and stood up. He beckoned the woman over and spoke to Grey Owl.

'White Bear ask you to stand,' Grey Owl said.

The three of us stood and the squaw looked us over. While she spoke she pointed to her eye then ran her finger down the left side of her cheek. White Bear said something else and again the woman spoke and indicated her eye and her cheek. White Bear turned to Grey Owl and spoke again. Grey Owl turned to us.

'White Bear say you speak the truth,' he said. 'Little Feather here say there were four men. Two young and dark-skinned. Two older. One younger man have scar on side of face. One of the older men have one eye that look the wrong way.'

'A squint?' Ben asked.

'Yes, a squint,' Grey Owl replied.

'What did these men do? I asked. 'What happened?'

'Three squaws and two children down at river, get water,' Grey Owl said. 'Men ride up and man with scar get off horse and take younger squaw to long grass. He pull up dress, start to rape her. Older squaw, she mother, take stone and hit his head. He turn, take pistol and shoot her. Young squaw scratch his face and he shoot her too. Little Feather take children and run. Other men take their pistols and shoot at Little Feather and children. All fall, but Little Feather not hit, only knocked out.'

'Were the children kin to the murdered woman?' I asked.

'Yes,' Grey Owl replied. 'Her son and her daughter. Her husband, Lone Wolf's brother, was killed in buffalo hunt three years ago. Now all his family is gone.'

'I'm sorry,' Ben said.

White Bear spoke, then Grey Owl translated:

'He say you all free to leave but asks that you sit with him and take drink first, it is custom.'

We again sat in our places. Little Feather took a pot from the fire and poured herb tea into clay cups, which she passed around. White Bear then spoke at length, and Grey Owl translated.

'White Bear asks you to forgive us, but hopes you will understand why you were brought here. His heart is heavy after the killings of Lone Wolf's brother's wife and her mother and children. All the tribe are angry, but he says he knows this anger must be tempered with reason. Many among us have wish to go on warpath and take scalps in revenge.

'But White Bear say if we do this we no better than the men who carry out this deed. So he ask the young men to cool their tempers and have patience. He says he believes eventually the Great Spirit will reveal who the guilty men are. He also says he knows there are good as well as bad among white people, and that to make innocent suffer because of these deeds of the guilty would be wrong.'

'What happened is a helluva thing,' I said. 'I can understand your anger.'

'I agree,' Ben said. He took a sip of his tea, put down the cup, and looked at our interpreter. 'Grey Owl, do you mind if I ask a question?'

'No. Ask.'

'You were headed in the direction of Las Cruces when you found us. Weren't you following the men's trail?'

'Yes, we follow,' Grey Owl replied. 'But we not return from hunt until early this morning. Heavy rains fall overnight and in many places it wash away tracks. We follow till Twin Buttes. Find no trace after.'

'Well, Wes and I are headed to El Paso now,' Ben said. 'Perhaps we could stop off at Fort Bliss? The military might send a patrol to search for these men.'

White Bear asked for a translation, then gave his answer.

'He say no,' Grey Owl said. 'The bluecoats do not want to have dealings with the Apache and we do not want dealings with them. The leaders among them treat us as inferior and wish us to leave our ancestral lands, as many of our people have already done. White Bear says patience is the answer. He has faith we will find the men who did this. He thanks you for your offer, and hopes you will go in peace.'

An hour later we were back on the trail again. The Apaches had returned our weapons and given Bannister a pony in compensation for the horse they'd shot from under him. We rode on to Twin Buttes, where we came back to the main trail running north and south. Although it was nearly three o'clock the air was still and the heat oppressive. Bannister reined his pony to a stop at the fork and wiped his neck with his kerchief.

'Damned if I can get used to riding a horse without a saddle,' he said.

Ben nodded towards Bannister's burro, which was trailing behind the pony on a rope.

'I'd say it's a darn sight better than riding your donkey.'

'Yeah, a couple of hours ago none of us knew if we'd be riding anywhere,' I said. Bannister shook his head.

'You fellas don't seem too upset. Them redskins came damn near to killing us.'

'I'd say we came out of it OK,' Ben replied. 'After what happened we were lucky to escape with our lives.'

'Christ, mister!' Bannister said, 'you're goddam blasé. Don't you realize – the minute those redskins discovered the killings they must've lit out to find white men? *Any* white men? Wouldn't it have been better if they'd asked the squaw to describe the killers *before* they started their rampage?'

Ben looked at Bannister for a long moment.

'Yeah, I reckon you could take that view,' he said. 'Or you could put yourself in their shoes. They come back from their hunt to find two women and two young 'uns shot dead. The younger squaw raped before being shot. The men's leader, one of the younger chiefs, is both an uncle and brother-in-law. The woman who witnessed the killing is near-hysterical, says the four men were white. Do you honestly mean to tell me in their place you'd stick around, get a more detailed description?'

Bannister blanched a little when he saw the anger in Ben's eyes.

19

'A man's entitled to his opinion.' He shrugged. He took the burro's rope and kicked the pony's flanks. 'Well, reckon I'll be seeing you. Gotta get back to where those redskins waylaid me. Look for the samples they cut from my pack animal. If I don't find them, I'll have to return to Silver City.'

I waited until Bannister had ridden away a short distance.

'Think he'd be glad to escape with his hair intact,' I said. Ben reined his bay gelding to the left and we began riding south.

'Yeah, his blood's up now,' he said. 'Almost shit himself when Grey Owl took out his knife.'

'Yeah, I noticed.' I took my bandanna and mopped sweat from my brow. 'Reckon the Apaches have a chance of finding the killers?'

'Been thinking on that. It's for certain Lone Wolf ain't gonna let it rest. Be surprised if he don't put out feelers to other Apaches bands in New Mexico. Texas, too, come to that. Big territory for these men to get lost in, of course. On the other hand they still might be in the area. Wouldn't like to be in their shoes if they are.'

CHAPTER THREE

We rode until the sun was low on the horizon. By then we reckoned we'd entered Texas, but figured we'd another ten miles to cover before we reached El Paso. Near sundown, we crested a ridge and saw a town on the southernmost edge of the plain beneath.

'Don't know about you, Wes,' Ben said, 'But I'm tuckered out.' He nodded towards the town. 'Reckon we could find us a place for the night, carry on to El Paso in the morning.'

Sally, my chestnut mare, had been blowing a lot harder for the last five miles.

'No argument from me, Ben,' I replied. 'Reckon the horses could use a feed and rest, too.'

We rode on and came to a board nailed to a post on the outskirts that told us the town was called

Copper Creek. The main street ran north to south; we walked the horses three-quarters of the way along and pulled up outside a livery stable.

As we dismounted and tethered our mounts a stocky man with a black beard got up from a chair on the stoop and walked over. He extended a hand.

'Evenin' gents. Lionel Sweet's the name,' he said, then he smiled and added, 'Sweet by name 'n' sweet by nature.' He nodded to a notice above the stable entrance. 'Like the sign says, "Hostler, Farrier and Blacksmith". Take care of your animals?'

'Appreciate if you would.' Ben shook his hand. 'My name's Ben Turner. My sidekick here's Wes Noble.'

'Pleased to meet you both.' Sweet said. 'Gonna be stayin' in Copper Creek long?'

'Just one night,' Ben replied. 'We're headed for El Paso in the morning.'

'I see. Got a place to stay?' Sweet asked.

'No,' Ben replied. 'I was gonna ask if you could recommend someplace.'

Sweet went to the hitching post and took the reins of our horses.

'Alamo's OK. A dollar a night with breakfast, I think. Less you're looking for something cheaper. Ma Porter's boarding house is at the corner of the last block.'

'A dollar a night'll suit us fine,' Ben said.

'The Alamo's two blocks down on your left. Tell Nick – Nick Carter, he's the proprietor – I sent you.'

We thanked Sweet and began walking down the street. As we approached the Alamo we saw a young woman with blonde hair step from the boardwalk and hitch up her skirts preparatory to crossing. As she stepped down two men came out of the saloon; one of them went over to her.

'Why, if it ain't pretty little Eliza from the general store,' he said. He took her arm. 'See you home, sweetheart?'

'No, please, I can manage. Let go of my arm.' The young woman looked surprised and frightened.

The man was around thirty, unshaven and in need of a wash. His partner was tall, rake-thin, and looked every bit as unkempt.

'Only talk to gentlemen when you're serving 'em in your daddy's store, huh? That it, sweetheart?'

'Please, please, let go my arm.'

The man nodded towards the Alamo.

'What about steppin' inside, honey? Have a little drink with Toby and me?'

A look of panic flashed over the woman's face.

'No! I want to go home. Please, let me go,' she said, her voice now almost a whimper.

'Why don't you do as the lady asks, mister?' Ben said.

The man kept hold of the woman and turned to see who had spoken. The sidekick called Toby turned round to face us and his hand went to his gunbelt. Ben drew back his coat in readiness and I did likewise.

'Who are you?' asked the man holding the woman.

'Ain't no concern of yours,' Ben replied. 'The lady said she wants you to let her go. You gonna mind your manners and do as she says?'

'Look, stranger, I don't see what this is to do with you. This conversation's between me and the lady here. Why don't you and your pal go where you're headed?' He straightened up and his right hand dropped to his waist. 'Before you wind up with a bullet.'

The woman screamed at that moment and the man loosened his grip. She broke free and bolted across the street to the general store. She opened the door and went inside. Her tormentor turned to Ben.

'Now look what you've gone and done. I almost persuaded that bitch to take a drink with me. Hell, I have might even gotten lucky.' He brought both hands level with his gunbelt, where they covered holsters carrying two Navy sixes. He sneered and rocked on his heels. 'Speaking of luck, mister . . . yours just ran out.'

He cleared leather as he spoke; his pistols were almost in a shooting position when a bullet from Ben's Colt hit his chest. A look of amazement came over his face, then his back arched and he crashed to the ground.

I had Toby covered, but he hadn't even palmed his pistol when he witnessed Ben's draw. His hand was frozen midway in the act of reaching for his weapon when he thought better of it and put his hands in the air. He cast Ben an awed look.

'Don't pull the trigger, mister. I ain't gonna draw.'

'Where're you from?' Ben asked.

'Ed Holden's ranch,' Toby replied. 'Lester Green and I work there.'

Ben waved the barrel of his pistol in the direction of the dead man.

'Is that Lester Green?'

Toby gave a strangled cough.

'Yeah,' he replied.

'Then you'd better string him over his mount and take him back for buryin'.'

We waited while Toby lifted the dead man and draped him over his horse. He mounted up and rode off at the gallop. He was soon lost in the gathering dusk.

Ben and I turned to the Alamo's swing doors and went inside, brushing past a group of men who'd witnessed the gunfight. Among them was a heavyset man around sixty years old.

'Helluva brave thing, mister,' he said. 'Not many men would've taken on one of Ed Holden's men.'

'Nothing else I could've done,' Ben said. 'He drew on me.'

'I know, I know,' the man said. 'My name's Nick Carter by the way, owner of the Alamo.' He gestured to the men behind him. 'All of us here saw what happened.'

Ben took off his Stetson and shook his head.

'A man pulls a pistol, he risks the consequences,' he said, wiping the headband with his bandanna. 'I'm Ben Turner. This here's my sidekick Wes Noble. Lionel Sweet, your hostler, told us you might have a couple of rooms for the night.'

'Sure thing, Mr Turner,' Carter replied. He waved to a nearby table. 'Can I buy you both a drink first?'

We accepted and sat at the table. He called to his barman, who brought over a bottle of Irish whiskey. Carter filled three shot glasses and put the bottle down.

'Here's to you both,' he said, raising his glass.

We returned the salutation and sipped the drink. I felt a pleasant warmth as the liquor hit the spot.

'You said you were staying just the one night?' asked Carter.

'That's right,' Ben replied. 'We plan on riding to El Paso in the morning.'

'Pardon my nose,' Carter was still curious, 'but you've got business there?'

Ben looked at me and I nodded. He answered for both of us.

'Don't mind. Wes and I are prospectors. Pan the Canadian, Red River too sometimes. Got us some ore to sell, reckon we'll get top dollar where we're headed.'

'You don't look like prospectors,' Carter said.

'What do prospectors look like?' asked Ben.

'Any've come through here are old men with a stoop to their gait, not tall young fellers like yourself and Mr Noble.'

Ben grinned. 'I guess we come in all shapes and sizes.'

'Well, if you're headed to El Paso just to sell ore you might save yourself a journey,' Carter said. 'Arthur Grace at the general store is an assayer. It was his daughter, Eliza who you rescued from Holden's rannie. I understand he pays a fair price for gold. Might give you a good deal. He opens at half past eight.'

CHAPTER FOUR

Just before nine the next morning Ben and I crossed the street to the general store. A brass bell on a spring clanged as we opened the door. A small bespectacled man with grey hair came out from the other side of a long counter and walked over.

' 'Morning, gentlemen,' he said. 'What can I get you?'

' 'Morning,' Ben replied. 'Are you Arthur Grace?'

'Yes, that's me.'

'Mr Carter at the Alamo told us you buy gold.'

'Yes, sir, I sure do. . . .'

At that moment the door of a back room opened and the woman who'd been the object of Lester Green's attentions the previous night walked in. She gasped in surprise when she saw Ben and me, then smiled and hurried to her father's side.

'Papa, these are the gentlemen who helped me escape the clutches of Lester Green last night,' she said. She looked at Ben. 'I'm sorry; I heard he tried to kill you and you had to shoot him. I was so distraught at the time – I had to get away. Papa and I went to the Alamo to thank you later, but Mr Carter told us you'd retired.'

Ben and I tipped our hats.

' 'Morning ma'am,' Ben said. 'That was kind of you. Sorry we missed you. Wes and I'd had a long ride; we were tuckered out. Mr Carter bought us a drink and we called it a day.'

The young woman smiled at Ben.

'Please, call me Eliza,' she said. 'Mr Carter told me your names. You're Ben Turner?'

'Yes, ma'am – sorry, Eliza,' Ben replied. She turned to me.

'And you're Wes Noble?'

I gave an affirming nod. 'Pleased to meet you, Eliza.'

Arthur Grace shook our hands warmly.

'What you did was no small thing, Mr Turner, and I want to tell you I'm very grateful indeed. Green was a particularly nasty individual, as are most of Ed Holden's men.'

'Yeah,' Ben said. 'The fella with Green told us

30

they worked at the Holden ranch.'

Grace raised his eyebrows.

'Wouldn't call it a ranch, Mr Turner. Holden took over the old Miller place two years ago. Wouldn't call what they do out there *work*, either. Holden has a gang of men who stay with him, unsavoury types – gunslingers like Green. Don't keep any livestock. He and his men live by their wits. Terrorize decent folks and live on what they can get by intimidating—'

Eliza cut in. 'Don't, Papa. Mr Turner and Mr Noble don't want to hear about the town's troubles.'

'It's OK, Eliza,' Ben said. 'Wes and I don't mind. Go ahead, Mr Grace.'

'Thing is, Mr Turner, Copper Creek has no law. Last man who served as marshal was injured trying to bring order. Faced down two men in a saloon fight and had a pistol shot from his hands. Rode to El Paso soon afterwards, said he couldn't take on the entire bunch.'

'What about the county sheriff?' I asked.

'He and a bunch of deputies ride though every month,' Grace answered. 'But Holden and his men are never here when he does. Nobody says anything about what goes on, of course. Frightened what'll happen if they do.'

'What goes on?' Ben asked. Grace looked at his daughter then back at Ben.

'Extortion, Mr Turner. Plain and simple. Not long after he bought the Miller place Holden and his cohorts began coming into my store. I welcomed them, of course. But soon he started settling his bills late, then stopped paying altogether.

'One day he and three of his men came in and bought fifty dollars' worth of supplies. When I said he'd have to pay cash until he cleared his account, he grew threatening, said I'd better give him the goods or take the consequences. I refused point blank and he left.

'That night my store was broken into and five hundred dollars' worth of goods was taken.'

'Holden and his gang?' Ben queried. Grace nodded.

'We never actually saw them. But the next day he and his men came in again. "Looks like you've been robbed," he said. The store was still a mess, but I didn't reply. "There's a way you can avoid this happening again," he said. "Me 'n my men'll protect your store. Cost you fifty dollars a week."

'I demurred, of course. But I knew he had me over a barrel. "You never know, next time your store might go up in smoke," he said. He gave a nod and one of his men struck a match, ostensibly to light his cigar, but the meaning was clear: *pay up or else.*'

'It's called a protection racket,' I said. 'Read about it a while ago. Been happening in some of the big cities back East.'

'Yeah, I read that, too,' Ben said. 'And you're payin' him?'

'I am, Mr Turner,' Grace replied. 'And I'm not the only one. Every business in Copper Creek does. We've had to; it's that or go under.'

Eliza had remained silent as her father spoke, but now she changed the subject.

'Please, Papa, These gentlemen have been burdened enough.' She turned to Ben. 'Mr Turner, when I came in did I hear you say you're looking to sell gold?'

'I – well, yes, you did, Eliza,' Ben replied. He took the gunny sack from his coat. 'Wes and I would like to ask what your father would offer us for this here ore. Reckon it's around five pounds in weight.'

'Of course, Mr Turner,' Grace replied. 'Sorry, I forgot; you mentioned it when you came in. Please, bring your sack over to the scales and we'll weigh it.'

We went with him and he placed the gold on a pair of scales in a teakwood cabinet. He adjusted the scales with a brass knob until he found the correct weight. He loosened the sack's drawstrings, gave the contents a cursory glance, then pulled the strings tight again.

'Four pounds, thirteen ounces,' Grace said. 'I pay the same as they do in El Paso, Mr Turner. Ten dollars an ounce. That'll give you seven hundred and seventy dollars.'

Ben looked at me and I nodded my agreement.

'That'll suit us fine, Mr Grace,' he said. 'We'll accept. You've saved us a ride to El Paso.'

Grace gave Ben and me a studied look.

'I'd like to make it a thousand, gentlemen,' he said. 'And offer a proposition I hope you'll find to your advantage.'

Ben shot me a quick glance and looked back at Grace.

'We're listening,' he said.

'I'm sixty-seven years old, Mr Turner.' Grace glanced at his daughter. 'Eliza and I have discussed this, so what I'm about to say'll come as no surprise to her. You see, I want to retire and I'd like to sell my business. I wonder if you and Mr Noble would consider buying it from me?'

'I can't speak for Wes, Mr Grace,' Ben replied, 'but I've no experience of running a store. 'Sides, your offer of a thousand dollars, generous though it is, wouldn't see us with anything near enough. Wes and I got no savings.'

'I'm aware prospecting's not always remunerative, Mr Turner. However lack of capital's not an issue. My turnover is around thirty thousand a year. The store, together with stock, is worth around fifteen thousand dollars—'

Ben interrupted. 'Sorry, Mr Grace,' he said. 'There's no way we could raise that kind of cash, even if we were interested.'

Grace held up his hand. 'Please, Mr Turner . . . please, hear me out.'

'OK,' Ben said. 'Go on.'

'I'm quite comfortably off,' Grace continued. 'Eliza and I have a nice house just a block from here and I've no other needs. The proposition I'd like to make to you gentlemen is this: I'll sell you the store for ten thousand dollars, based on a deposit of one thousand dollars, the remainder to be repaid interest-free over a period of five years. Eliza would inherit any balance if I die before the five years are up. Does that sound fair?'

'It does, Mr Grace,' replied Ben. 'But didn't you say the store was worth fifteen thousand?'

'Well, there's the ongoing problem with Holden,' said Grace. 'I reckon that devalues the business a little. On the plus side, the town's growing. There's increasing trade with local farmers and ranchers, not forgetting workers at the copper mine five miles outside town. I reckon the profits would guarantee you both a good living.'

'It's an attractive offer,' said Ben, then he turned to me. 'What do you think, Wes?'

'It is,' I replied. 'But, like you said, Ben, we got no experience of this line of work.'

'I'd be happy to work with you both for a while,' Eliza chipped in. 'Until you got to know the inventory.'

Grace nodded enthusiastically.

'There you go, gentlemen. Eliza helps me out when it's busy; she knows every item we stock.'

'We were planning on leaving this morning, Mr Grace,' Ben said. 'But your price for the gold means we'll stay a day longer. That'll give Wes and me time to discuss your proposition. Is it OK if we give you our answer tomorrow morning?'

'Why, of course, Mr Turner,' replied Grace.

He gave Ben the full amount he'd promised for the gold, then he and Eliza walked us to the door.

Outside on the boardwalk, Eliza smiled at us.

'I do hope you'll take up Papa's offer,' she said, then she looked at Ben. 'But, whatever you decide, I'm indebted to you for last night.'

CHAPTER FIVE

For the rest of the day Ben and I weighed up the pros and cons of Grace's proposition. It was certainly appealing: we'd spent six years since mustering out of the army, literally scratching a living, and didn't want to be doing the same in another ten years.

Neither of us was sure if we'd be successful as storekeepers, though. Then there was the balance of nine thousand, payable over five years.

On the other hand, with takings of thirty thousand each year, we figured it'd be easily met from profits, assuming twenty per cent of gross. We reckoned that that would see us each with a weekly clear income of around forty bucks, which was a darn sight more than we made separating gold dust from muddy water.

We stayed at the Alamo a second night. At breakfast the following morning we were still discussing Grace's offer when we were interrupted by Nick Carter, who came rushing into the dining room.

'Mr Turner,' he said, 'Ed Holden and his men are coming up the street. I think they're looking for you.'

'How many of them are there?' asked Ben.

'Not really sure,' Carter replied. 'Maybe a dozen.'

'Thanks,' said Ben. 'When they come in tell them we're in the lounge.'

Ben and I took up our rifles; a minute later we were sitting at separate tables in the lounge, myself next to a back wall with a good view of the window and door, and Ben at a corner table, where he was able to cover the same entry points from a different angle.

After some moments we heard the sound of voices in the lobby, then the lounge door swung open.

Ed Holden walked in with five men at his back. The jangle of his spurs sounded muffled as he crossed the thick carpet and stood to face Ben.

'I'm Ed Holden,' he said.

'Ben Turner,' Ben replied. 'This here's Wes Noble.'

38

Holden looked at me. I gave a nod, then I looked through the window and saw five other men standing at the Alamo's entrance. Holden pointed to our rifles.

'Looks like you've been expecting me,' he said.

'Always like to be prepared,' replied Ben. Holden pushed back his Stetson.

'You shot one of my men Sunday night.'

'That I did,' Ben said.

'Man who was there says Green was talking to a woman and you called him out.'

'Did the man tell you Green was giving the lady grief?' asked Ben. 'That I told him to leave her be, and he wouldn't? That when she'd managed to drag herself free Green pulled his pistols on me?'

'Toby says you drew first.'

'Toby's a liar.'

Holden was tall, his weathered face sported a pencil moustache. His gunbelt was made of tooled leather with fancy stitching and in his holster was a Colt Peacemaker with ivory grips. He stroked his chin and looked straight at Ben.

'You planning on leaving town, Mr Turner?'

Ben held eye contact. 'We ain't made our minds up yet.'

'Thing is, after what happened, things might not be too healthy around here.'

'Oh? How do you figure that?'

'Well, maybe I'm prepared to accept your version of what happened Sunday.' Holden gestured with his thumb to the five behind him. 'Can't say the same for my men.'

'You reckon if we leave they might forget what happened,' Ben said.

'Something like that.'

'Then we may have to disappoint you.'

'You mean you're staying?'

'We're in no great hurry to leave.'

'What possible business could you have in Copper Creek?' Holden said. 'I heard you were prospectors on your way to El Paso.'

Ben looked at me and winked.

'We were, but now we're staying.'

'To do what?'

'Not that it's any business of yours, Mr Holden. But Wes and I are buying the general store. We're gonna become storekeepers.'

'Old man Grace's place? I didn't know he was selling.'

'You're not as well informed as you thought you were.'

'Stay in town and I can't guarantee my men'll leave you be,' Holden said.

Ben glanced through the window, then looked

back at Holden and smiled.

'Wes 'n' I have faced worse odds.'

Holden inclined his head.

'Of course,' he said. 'I shoulda had you both pegged sooner. You're ex-army regulars. You were with some kinda sharpshooter outfit in the war, right? Frémont? Carpenter's Jessie Scouts? You must be good to have been able to clear leather 'fore Green.'

'Good enough,' said Ben. 'That's all that matters.'

Holden looked at us and sneered.

'OK,' he said. 'I'll take my leave. But a little friendly advice before I go: my men ain't gonna let this matter over Green drop. If I was you, I'd watch how I went about my business.'

It was a little after ten when we called in at the general store. Grace was helping a customer carry sacks of feed to a buckboard outside when he saw us.

'Just go inside, gentlemen,' he said. 'Eliza's there. I'll be back in a minute.'

We went inside and saw Eliza taking cans from a box and putting them on a shelf. She looked up and smiled.

'Good morning Mr Turner, Mr Noble. I'm

delighted to see you again.'

'Please, Eliza; Turner and Noble's way too formal,' Ben said. 'I'm Ben, he's Wes.'

Eliza closed the box and came out from behind the counter. She gave a little laugh.

'OK, Ben, Wes. You've decided to take Papa's offer?'

'Yes, Eliza, we have.'

She clasped her hands and beamed.

'Oh, I'm so glad,' she said. 'I was hoping you'd stay.' She indicated a stove near the window. 'I was just about to make coffee. You'll both have a cup, of course?'

'Thank you, yes,' Ben replied.

Grace came back into the store then and walked up to us.

'Did I hear you tell Eliza you're going to stay?' he said. 'You'll accept my proposition?'

'Yes, Mr Grace,' Ben replied. 'We will.'

'Excellent, excellent,' said Grace. 'You can take over as soon as you wish. I'll remain for a day or two if you like, to show you the accounts, paperwork, etcetera. Eliza will stay as long as you need her after that, till you get the hang of stock and prices.'

'Well, we've just a few hundred dollars over and above the deposit,' Ben told him 'So we reckon we'd better get earning soon. Got our room and board to pay at the Alamo.'

'No need for you to stay there, Ben.' Grace said. 'There's a big room and kitchen at the back of the store. Myself, my wife and Eliza used it before we had our house built. There are beds and other items of furniture, and a stove. Outhouse, too, at the back. I'll sign the business over to you today, and you can both move in. Start in the store tomorrow, if that's OK?'

'That would be fine.' Ben looked at me and I nodded.

Eliza came over with a tray of coffee; we each took a cup and sat at a table. Grace took a briar pipe from his vest pocket, lit it and puffed until he got it going, then pointed the stem in the direction of the Alamo.

'I gather you had a visit from Holden this morning.'

'Yes, we did,' replied Ben.

'He threaten you?'

'Not directly. He and his men's noses are a little out of joint about what happened to Green.'

'But he *did* threaten you, Ben?' Eliza repeated.

'He made some comments that were less than neighbourly,' Ben told her. 'But Wes and I ain't gonna lose any sleep.'

'But you'll be careful?' Eliza said. 'Holden's a

dangerous thug.'

'Wes and I have been threatened before, Eliza. Most times it don't come to anything.' Ben put down his cup and turned back to address Eliza's father.

'This fifty dollars' protection money, Mr Grace, When're you due to pay it next?'

Grace tapped the ash from his pipe into an old coffee can lid that served as an ashtray.

'Holden gets two of his men to collect. Usually around noon on Fridays.'

'Hmm, three days,' Ben said. 'Well, I think he's gonna be disappointed this week.'

'It might be risky, Ben,' Grace said. 'But—'

'Isn't it worth paying the fifty dollars, Ben?' Eliza interrupted. 'Holden hinted that he would resort to arson if Papa didn't pay.'

'As your father said yesterday, Eliza,' Ben replied, 'it's extortion. Plain and simple. Time it was put a stop to.'

CHAPTER SIX

Ben and I kept busy over the next two days, getting to know the ins and outs of the business. Grace kept an extensive inventory for his customers, who came from anywhere up to ten miles away to buy. Popular items we had to price included saddles, chaps, spurs, branding irons, weapons and clothing. On the farming and domestic side there were spades, hoes, rakes, brushes, all kinds of cutlery and crockery, and any number of pots and pans.

There was also an extensive stock of tinned and bulk groceries, animal feeds and a fair selection of sweetmeats and confectionery. Eliza told us that altogether we carried 800 individual items. Anything we didn't have could be chosen from

pictures and descriptions in any of the three cata-
logues on the counter. When a customer bought
from these the order was wired to the company
back East and a teamster delivered, usually within
three weeks.

On the Thursday after we took over Grace's business Ben was out front helping a customer load
sacks from the boardwalk on to a wagon and Eliza
was in the storeroom. I was on my own tending the
counter when a dark-haired young woman came in
with a boy aged around five years.

'Good morning,' she said. 'Is Mr Grace or his
daughter in?'

'Good morning, ma'am,' I replied. 'Mr Grace
has retired. But Eliza's out back, I can get her if
you'd like.'

'I didn't know Mr Grace had retired.'

'No, ma'am, you wouldn't. It's just recent. My
friend and I only bought the store on Tuesday.'

'Oh, I see. And Eliza's still here?'

'Yes, ma'am. She helping us until we get to know
the inventory. We're completely new to the business.'

The woman's hair spilled over her shoulders and
framed a pretty face. She wore a blue velvet dress
complete with lace trimmings and matching
bonnet. I noticed, too, that her figure was nicely

proportioned.

'Perhaps you can help me, Mr. . . ?' she said.

'Noble, ma'am. Wes Noble.'

She smiled. 'Pleased to meet you, Mr Noble. My name's Abigail Doherty, I'm a friend of Eliza's. It's about some cloth I ordered from the Montgomery Ward catalogue. I was wondering if it had arrived.'

I took the catalogue order book from the drawer.

'Let me take a look for you. Is it Miss Doherty or Mrs Doherty?'

'Mrs,' she replied. I thumbed through the pages.

'Yes, here we are,' I said. 'Mrs A. Doherty, one bolt of silk cloth, colour: blue. It should be in the storeroom. I'll get it for you.'

'Thank you,' she said.

I went through to the storeroom and checked the shelves where the catalogue orders were kept. Eliza was labelling crockery and she glanced over.

'Find what you're looking for, Wes?' she asked.

'Not yet, Eliza,' I replied. 'It's an order for a bolt of silk. For Mrs Abigail Doherty.'

'Cloth orders are on the second top shelf, Wes. Abby still out front?'

'Yes. She's got a little boy with her.'

'That's her son, Tommy. I must go and say hello.'

I went to the shelf, found the order, and when I returned Eliza was holding Tommy in her arms.

'Aren't you a little darling?' she said, playfully pinching his cheeks. Tommy chuckled and pointed to a jar on the counter.

'Can I have a stick of candy, Eliza?'

Eliza gave Abigail an enquiring look. 'Can he, Abby?'

Abigail patted her son's head. 'Only if you promise to eat all your vegetables at dinner tonight,' she replied.

'I promise,' said Tommy.

I took Abigail's cloth to the counter and wrapped it.

'Will you give Tommy a piece of candy, Wes?' Eliza said. 'I'll pay you later.'

I opened the candy jar and winked at Tommy. I gave him a piece, then put four more in a paper bag and handed them to Abigail.

'He can have these another time,' I said. I grinned at Eliza. 'No charge,' I added.

'Oh, Mr Noble, you shouldn't really,' Abigail said. 'Eliza's got him spoiled enough as it is.'

'Please, ma'am, it's my pleasure.'

'Well, that's really very kind of you, Mr Noble – and please call me Abby. All my friends do.'

'Be glad to, Abby. My friends call me Wes.'

'OK – Wes.' She smiled coquettishly and reached for her purse. 'Now, what do I owe you for the cloth?'

A short while later when Abby had settled up and left the store, Eliza said, 'You know, Wes, I think you've an admirer.'

I suddenly felt self-conscious.

'You can't mean Mrs Doherty, Eliza, she's a married woman.'

'She's been widow for almost six years, Wes. Her husband died before Tommy was born.'

'She doesn't look old enough to have been widowed six years. How did her husband die?'

'Abby's twenty-seven. Four years older than me. Luke Doherty was a drover with an outfit on the Western Trail. He was killed in a stampede.'

'Must have been tough on her. Particularly with a youngster.'

'It was at first. But Abby's got spirit. She got through it OK. She supports herself and Tommy making dresses. She's good at it, too. Runs her business from home – most women in Copper Creek are her customers.'

'Quite a lady,' I said.

At that moment Ben came into the store, his shirt soaked from his exertions.

'Eliza, Wes,' he said. 'You'll have to excuse me, I'll need to go change my shirt. Worked up quite a sweat toting those feed sacks.'

'There's a pitcher of lemonade in the storeroom, Ben,' Eliza told him. 'I'll fetch it through. You can have a glass when you get back.'

'That'll be just fine, Eliza. I've worked up quite a thirst, too.'

'Wes and I were discussing Abby Doherty, the woman who just left,' Eliza said.

'The lady with the boy?'

'Yes.' Eliza's eyes remained on Ben. 'Papa and I have invited her to lunch on Sunday. We'd like you and Wes to come, too.'

'Never could refuse a home cooked meal,' Ben replied.

'Me neither,' I said.

'Good, then it's settled.'

Eliza smiled and went to get the lemonade.

Holden's henchmen came into the store before noon the next day. I'd just sold some Bull Durham tobacco to a couple of miners and was putting the money in the cash drawer. Eliza had gone to get lunch for her father, and Ben was halfway up a ladder stacking paint on a shelf near the door.

The two walked in just as the miners left. The first man through the door was of medium height and ruddy complexion His sidekick was tall and heavily built, with a square jaw and a bulbous nose. Both men carried new Schofield .44-calibres, holstered low on their gunbelts.

Ben saw the pair enter and got down from the ladder.

'Help you, gentlemen?' he asked.

'Newton McKenna,' the shorter man said. He gestured to his companion. 'This is Silas Burnett. Hear tell you're the store's new owners.'

'You hear correct,' Ben replied.

'We work for Ed Holden,' McKenna said. 'Come to collect the overseein' money.'

'What overseein' money?'

'Money we get for protectin' your property,' McKenna said.'

'We don't need no protecting. We're able to look after ourselves.'

'Old Mr Grace paid it.'

'Mr Grace has retired,' Ben told him. Burnett's hand went to his holster.

'You gonna be difficult, we can be, too,' he said.

I'd taken my Henry from under the counter and had it aimed at his belly.

'That wouldn't be a smart move, mister,' I said, then I motioned with the barrel. 'Hands in the air, both of you.'

51

Burnett and McKenna turned their heads in surprise. I thought they'd spotted me when they came in, but it appeared their attention had been focused on Ben.

Burnett reacted to the barrel of the Henry, but only by moving his hands a fraction from his gunbelt. McKenna responded faster and raised his arms in the air.

'I said "reach",' I repeated to Burnett. He brought his arms up level with McKenna's.

'Don't either of you stir an inch,' Ben said. 'I'm gonna unbuckle your gunbelts.' He nodded to me. 'Wes's rifle's got a hair trigger. Move and he's liable to take your head off.'

I kept the Henry trained on Burnett and McKenna while Ben took their gunbelts and placed them on the counter.

'You came into our store extorting money with menaces,' he said. 'You aware that's against the law?'

McKenna scowled. 'There's no law in this town, 'cept Mr Holden's. All the merchants pay to have their premises protected. Don't hear them complain.'

'The merchants cough up because they're frightened of what'll happen if they don't. Holden's running an extortion racket and you're helping

52

him do it.'

'Tough, ain't it?' Burnet sneered. 'Who's gonna stop us? You?'

'Maybe. Meantime you can get your asses outta here. You come back, I can't guarantee we'll treat you so civil.'

'What about our pistols? Them's brand-new Schofields.'

Ben took one of the guns from its holster and examined it.

'Pretty fancy engraving,' he said. 'Must've set you back a few bucks.'

'Bought 'em in Silver City only recently,' said McKenna. 'Thirty-five dollars each. Gonna give us them back? You can empty the chambers.'

'No, I don't think I will,' Ben spun the gun on his forefinger. 'You came in here, armed, with the intention of extortion. Now Wes and I will do a little extorting of our own. We'll keep 'em. Think of it as a fine for your threatening behaviour. Might teach you a lesson.'

Burnett started to move and I raised my rifle.

'Another inch and I'll ventilate you in the bread basket,' I said. Burnett stopped.

'Helluva tough fella when you've a gun on a man,' he said.

Ben straightened up and looked him straight in

the eye.

'I don't need a gun, Burnett,' he said. 'McKenna, keep your hands in the air and move over beside Wes.'

McKenna edged to the counter and I kept him covered.

Ben approached Burnett. The man threw a left-hander. Ben dodged to his right and Burnett's paw clawed the air. Ben then jinked to the left and drove a fist into Burnett's stomach. He folded. Ben brought up his knee and connected with the big man's nose; it burst like a ripe tomato, blood streaming down his chin.

Ben swung the now inert Burnett around, lifted him by his collar, then grabbed the seat of his pants and propelled him to the door. Burnett had barely managed to put his feet to the boardwalk when his legs gave way and he dropped to the dirt of the street.

Ben came back inside and grabbed McKenna's shirtfront.

'Want some of the same, McKenna?'

McKenna shook his head and raised his hands in a gesture of appeasement.

'No, mister,' he said. 'I'm going.'

Ben escorted him to the door and shoved him on to the boardwalk.

'Any of you come near this store again, we ain't gonna be so lenient. Make sure you tell Holden.'

CHAPTER SEVEN

'Spoke to Lionel Sweet this morning,' Arthur Grace said. 'Tells me he saw a couple of Holden's men ride out of town on Friday. The taller of the two had a bloody nose.'

Ben and I were seated with Abby and Eliza and her father around a big oak table in their parlour at lunchtime the following Sunday. We had just finished a substantial meal and were now on the coffee.

Ben and I said nothing in reply; Grace stirred his cup. He looked at us quizzically.

'They call into the store?'

'Yes, they did,' I said. 'Ben and the big fella had a disagreement.'

'I thought as much.' Grace smiled. 'Asked for money and came away empty handed, eh? Didn't think you boys would give in to their demands.'

An anxious look came over Eliza's face. She looked at Ben.

'Aren't you worried they'll try something?'

'We've thought on it some, Eliza,' Ben replied. 'We don't fool ourselves for a minute that that'll be the end of it. But, like I said on Tuesday, we won't to give in to extortion. Don't worry. We're on the premises now, so there's less chance of arson. For that to succeed they'd have to get close. They do, we'll hear them or see them.'

'They'd be most likely to come at night,' said Eliza. 'When you're asleep.'

'Wes and I figured that possibility,' replied Ben. 'We've rigged some chicken wire around the back fence, tied to tin cans with pebbles. The slightest movement and they'll rattle. Besides, we're light sleepers. Habit from our time in the army.'

'Eliza told me about the troubles with Holden,' Abby joined in 'It's terrible no one will say anything.'

'People will put up with anything for a while, Abby,' I told her. 'But there's always a breaking point.'

'You're right, Wes,' Grace agreed. 'And I don't think it'll be long till it's reached.' He took his pipe from his vest pocket, lit it, then took a couple of puffs. 'Were you boys in the army?'

'Yes,' replied Ben. He put his cup down. 'We were both regulars. I was with Major General Dodge in Wyoming just before the war, and Wes was with Sheridan in Texas. We met up just before the Battle of Wilson's Creek. Mustered out in sixty-eight.'

'Heard Wilson's Creek was quite a fight.'

'Three hundred killed on the Union side,' I said. 'Confederates lost almost as many.'

'Oh, please, Papa,' said Eliza. 'Ben and Wes might not want to talk about their war experiences.'

'Sorry, Eliza,' Grace replied. 'I was just interested.'

'It's OK, we don't mind,' Ben said. 'What about yourself, Mr Grace? Been out here long?'

'Arrived with my wife Mary in eighteen-fifty. Year before Eliza was born. Nothing much here then except a miner's camp and a collection of tents. But I saw the possibilities and decided to put down roots. Hard life in the beginning. Didn't help Mary's lung condition.'

'Mother died when I was sixteen,' Eliza explained. 'Just after Papa built this house.'

'I remember,' Abby said. 'Mrs Grace died the year Luke and I arrived.'

'Of course,' Grace said. 'Didn't you and Luke arrive in sixty-seven?'

'Yes.' Abby turned to me and smiled. 'My husband was in the army, too, Wes. We married soon after he left. We came here and he got a job in the copper mine. But he didn't like working in confined spaces and left after two years to become a drover. He was killed in a stampede on his first cattle drive.'

'I'm sorry.'

'I'm OK now,' Abby continued, 'though I was devastated at the time. Didn't know how I was going to survive, either, what with Tommy due and no means of support. But everyone in Copper Creek – Mr Grace and Eliza especially – were very kind. They helped me through a particularly difficult time.'

'Eliza told me you were a dressmaker,' I said.

'Yes,' Abby replied. 'Nothing very *haute couture*, though.'

'You're far too modest, Abby,' said Eliza. 'She makes marvellous dresses, Wes. All the women in town think so.'

'Shush, Eliza.' Abby lowered her head. 'You're going to make me blush.'

'Speaking of dresses, Abby,' Eliza added, oblivious, 'I forgot to mention. A delivery of pink satin came for you yesterday.'

'It did?' Abby looked surprised. 'I'm sorry – I'll

not manage to pick it up until Tuesday. Dora, my neighbour, is sitting withTommy for me today. I've promised to reciprocate by looking after her youngest tomorrow. She'll be visiting her sister in El Paso.'

'That's not a problem, Abby,' Eliza assured her. 'Wes will bring it over for you. Won't you, Wes?'

'Huh? Oh, yes,' I replied. 'I'd be delighted.'

'Eliza wasn't very subtle in her attempts at match-making yesterday, was she?' Abby remarked. I was standing at the door of her neat little clapboard house at ten the following morning with her package of satin.

I grinned.

'No, I suppose she wasn't.'

'Come in, Wes, please. Got time for a coffee?'

'I'd appreciate one, thanks. The store's not busy at the moment.'

We went in to the living room and I saw a crib positioned near the window.

'That's Ella, my neighbour Dora King's youngest,' said Abby. 'She's sleeping. Don't worry, I don't think we'll wake her.' She indicated one of two easy chairs over by the hearth. 'Take a seat, Wes. Coffee's on the stove. Won't be a minute.'

She went through to the kitchen and reappeared

a minute later with a tray, which she placed on a low table.

'I just baked some cookies. Please help yourself.'

She sat opposite me and pulled the table nearer, then took a silver pot from the tray and poured coffee for both of us. She handed me a cup and took one herself.

'How's Tommy?' I asked.

'He's fine. He's over at the schoolhouse this morning. Miss Lane, his teacher, brings him back before noon.'

'Nice-looking young fella.'

'I can't take the credit for that, I'm afraid.' Abby smiled wistfully. 'He favours his father.'

'I hope you don't mind me asking. Why didn't Luke try to find some other kind of work here in Copper Creek? Must've been a bit of a wrench for you when he left.'

'I don't mind you asking. You're right, I wasn't all that happy being on my own. But I was aware that Luke had a restless nature.' She turned her cup so that the handle faced her.

'Soon after we met and married in Baltimore he told me he'd a hankering to go West. He said fortunes were being made and we would become rich. He was particularly taken with a notice he'd seen in the *Baltimore Sun* early in 1867. The advertisement said a wagon train was leaving town for California, where acres of farming land were being offered to settlers willing to cultivate the soil and grow fruit. So we took what money we had, bought a wagon, and loaded our belongings.'

'But you never got that far?'

'No, we didn't. A man joined the train soon after we left Kansas. Luke fell into conversation with him and he told Luke that huge ranches were being created in Texas, which was where he was headed. He said many longhorn cows ranged free, and a fortune could be made rounding them up and herding them north.

'We diverted to Texas, but we discovered that most of the so-called free-range cattle had already been branded.' Abby took a sip of coffee and put the cup back on the saucer.

'By then, of course, our money had dwindled almost to nothing. Luckily, Luke heard that men were being hired to mine copper near El Paso. So we packed up immediately and made our way here.'

'But couldn't Luke have found other work in Copper Creek?'

'Sorry, Wes, I didn't really answer your question.' Her face took on a wistful look, then she nodded her head.

'Yes, he probably could have. But, like I say, he

was restless. I don't think he was ever happy in one place for any length of time. Only a few months before Tommy was born a foreman for one of the big cattle outfits came to town and offered him a job droving. It was plain to see he was delighted to be on the move again.'

'Did you hear from him again before the accident?'

'No. I didn't know anything until one of his trail mates called in on his way to San Antonio and broke the news. He told me Luke's body had been badly mauled and it had been decided to bury him in Amarillo, near where the stampede occurred.'

I could see tears welling up in her eyes as she spoke.

'I'm sorry,' I said. 'I shouldn't have asked. It was insensitive.'

'No, Wes, it's OK.' Abby placed her hand on mine. 'Honestly.'

I put down my empty cup and stood up.

'Well, Abby, I enjoyed the coffee very much,' I said. 'But I'd better be getting back.'

'It was kind of you to bring my satin, Wes, I really appreciate it.'

'My pleasure.'

She walked me to the door, and I decided to say how I felt about her.

'I've a confession to make, Abby. I'm glad Eliza suggested it. I really wanted to see you again.'

She took me by the shoulders and kissed my cheek.

'I wanted to see you too, Wes.'

'Great,' I said. 'Would you and Tommy like to go on a picnic Thursday? The store closes early and I can borrow the buggy.'

'Why of course, I'd be delighted. I'm sure Tommy would be, too.'

'Great. Three o' clock be OK?'

'Three would be fine, Wes. I'll bring some chicken and cold cuts of ham.'

'That's kind of you, Abby. I'll bring wine and some soda pop for Tommy.'

CHAPTER EIGHT

Our rooms were in a small annexe tacked on to the back of the store. They comprised a parlour with a small recess that served as a kitchen, a large bedroom and a boxroom. A door at the rear of the parlour led to the yard.

At eleven next evening I'd just put coffee on when I heard the distinct sound of cans rattling. I stood back from the stove for a moment, listened more intently, then heard it again. As I reached for my rifle the door opened and Ben came in.

'Only me,' he said. 'Just checking our alarm was OK.'

'Hell, Ben! You scared the bejesus outta me. Thought Holden's men had come to pay us a visit.'

'Sorry, Wes.' Ben grinned. 'I saw Eliza home then walked up the alley. Too much of a nuisance to open the store and come in at the front.'

'So, how was the stereo optical show at Mason's place?'

Ben corrected me. 'Stere*opticon*. Mason's got it set up at the back of his restaurant. Rows of chairs facing a white sheet. He calls it a screen. There's a big box near the back with two lenses that look a bit like binoculars. He puts glass squares into the box – slides, he calls them – and pictures are thrown on to the screen.'

'What did they show?'

'Niagara Falls at Lake Ontario on the American-Canadian border. It's really something to see, Wes. Mason calls it one of the world's wonders, and I believe him. Shaped like a horseshoe. He says it's a hundred and sixty feet high. Nine million gallons of water run over it every minute.'

'Sounds amazing,' I said, and poured coffee into two big mugs. 'You and Eliza have a meal at Mason's place afterward?'

'Yeah, we had steak, potatoes and fried onions followed by home-made apple pie,' Ben patted his stomach and added, 'Full fit to bust.' He picked up his mug and winked. 'Room for a coffee, though.'

'Sounds like you're getting kinda fond of Eliza.'

'Yeah, Wes, reckon I am. Ain't you and Abby got a thing going, too?'

'Tell the truth, Ben, I ain't met no one like her.'

'You and me ain't ever had real female company, have we? 'Less you count those sportin' gals we've visited in Las Cruces and Silver City.'

'Nice enough women, but Eliza and Abby are in a different class.'

'I know. I never thought I'd say this, Wes, but I've got a hankering to settle down. Maybe it's because I never felt secure before. Moneywise, I mean. This past few years we've only been just getting by. Now we've got the store . . . .'

'Yeah,' I agreed. 'I'll be thirty-nine if I see my next birthday. Gotta sudden urge to put down roots. New feeling for me, too.'

'But there's always a fly in the ointment.' Ben's brow furrowed and he gave a deep sigh.

'Holden and his cronies?'

'Exactly. Thought we'd have seen him by now after what happened on Friday.'

'Think he'll be content to bilk the other merchants and leave us be?'

'Not likely, Wes. Don't figure him for the type. We backed him down in front of his men and I don't think that sat well with him. No, I'm sure he's calculating the angles. Waiting his chance.'

'What about the county sheriff? We could send him a wire.'

'Yeah, Wes, I thought on that. Thing is, you and I could face him if he does come at us. Not sure about Copper Creek's other merchants.'

'You mean if the sheriff tried to arrest him and he bolted? He'd maybe return and exact revenge?'

'Just that. On the other hand, I think that sooner or later the merchants will have to make a stand. Maybe you and I can persuade them to do it sooner.'

The next day was the hottest we'd experienced. All the store's windows and doors were open, but this brought little relief as the air was so still.

By noon Ben and I had changed our shirts three times, yet each time we did so they were soaked again in minutes. Eliza made lemonade to help keep us cool but, although we got through two flagons, by noon we felt almost melted.

A little after twelve Eliza got ready to go and prepare her father's lunch, as she did every day.

'Ben, why don't you and Wes close up and go to the Alamo for a spell?' she suggested. 'The store's quiet now and it's likely to remain that way until one. I know Mr Carter took a delivery of ice this morning, so the beer's bound to be cold.'

'Good idea, Eliza,' replied Ben. 'Think I will. You, Wes?'

'Be just the ticket.' I licked my lips in anticipa-
tion.

We locked up after Eliza had left and crossed the
street. The saloon was empty except for Nick Carter
and O'Donnell, his barman.

'Good day to you Ben, Wes,' Carter said. 'Hot,
ain't it?'

'Hotter than Hades,' Ben replied. 'A lot cooler in
here, though.'

'That's the ice,' said Carter. 'Took a double delivery this morning.' He waved a hand towards the rest
of the room. 'Got three iceboxes strategically
placed,' he said. 'Makes a big difference.'

O'Donnell reached up, picked up two glasses,
then bent to the pump.

'No need to ask what you'll be having,' he said
with a smile. 'Two beers, is it, gentlemen?'

'Sounds fine to me,' replied Ben.

'You can fetch up another four while you're at it.'
The voice came from behind, and sounded harsh.

We turned and saw four men standing just inside
the swing doors. The speaker was of a dark complexion and had a scar on his cheek. He bore a
strong resemblance to the man nearest him, who
was of a similar age, around twenty-five.

He and his companions moved out of the shadow
of the doorway and walked to the bar. The other

two looked ten years older and were more heavily built, and I noticed that one of them had a boss eye. The man who had spoken put some coins on the counter and spoke again.

'Hurry it up, will you? We've ridden all the way from El Paso today. Got us a helluva thirst.'

O'Donnell made short work of pouring our beers, then he poured four more, which he placed in front of the men. Carter mumbled something about checking the cellar and left hurriedly.

Scarface lifted his glass and took a long swallow; then he wiped his mouth with a sleeve.

'Damn good,' he said. 'What a day, huh? Hotter than a two-bit whore on the Fourth of July.' He looked at the barman.

'Hey, Irish,' he said, 'we're looking for a fella called Ed Holden. Got a ranch near here. Know him?'

'Three miles south-west of town,' O'Donnell replied. 'Right fork near a grove of shinnery oaks.'

'Damnation!' Scarface swore. 'We passed that on our way into town.' He spat on the floor, then looked at Ben and me for a moment or two. 'You fellas from these parts?'

'Not really,' Ben replied. 'You?'

'Hell, no!' He nodded to his lookalike. 'Clem and me are from Kansas. We're twins. I'm Clay

70

Bonney. Maybe you've heard of me?'

'Can't say I have.' Ben took a swig of his beer. Bonney thumbed in the direction of the older men.

'Other two are Lenny Black and Claude Moresby. Don't suppose you've heard of them either?'

'Any reason I should have?'

'No, perhaps not.' Bonney adjusted his gunbelt. 'We're kinda like lawmen. Go where there's trouble. Some people say we're men to be feared.'

'That why you're headed to see Holden?'

'Right,' Bonney replied. 'He's got a problem with some of the folks here in Copper Creek. Hired us to sort it out.'

'Holden give you the name of the folks he's having trouble with?'

'Nope. Just wired to say he needed our help.'

The man with the boss eye studied Ben for a moment.

'You seem mighty interested, mister,' he said. 'Maybe you know the folks Holden's having trouble with?'

'Maybe,' Ben replied. 'But then again maybe not. We only arrived in town last week.'

'You see, Claude?' said Bonney. 'It's foolish to suspect everyone you meet.' He drank some more beer, then put down his glass.

'So what're your names, fellas?'

'I'm Ben Turner,' Ben replied. 'This here's my partner, Wes Noble.'

'Partner in what?' Bonney asked.

'We're storekeepers. Got us a place across the street.'

'First time I've seen storekeepers go about their business heeled,' said Moresby. He pointed to our gunbelts.

'Bit of a necessity in these parts,' Ben said. 'Never know when you're gonna run into trouble.'

Bonney's belly shook and he began to laugh.

'Hell, Mr Turner! You've an answer for everything.'

'Most things, I guess.' Ben smiled and gave me a nod. The affable look vanished from Bonney's face.

'Is there anything you don't have an answer for?'

'Well, now you mention it, there is,' said Ben. 'I was wondering if you fellas have run into any Apaches lately.'

Bonney frowned. 'Why'd you ask?'

'Because Wes and I were waylaid by a bunch of them on our way here. Tied us up and took us to their camp. Thought we might have been with the lowlifes who raped and killed a squaw and shot her mother and children. The chiefs let us go when another squaw who was there told them we weren't involved.'

Bonney stood away from the bar and the others moved to stay by him.

'This blanket-ass squaw say what the men looked like?' he asked.

Ben turned to face them all and I did likewise. O'Donnell pushed himself away from the counter and went down behind the bar.

'Two young men, one with a scar on his face,' said Ben. 'Two older fellas, one with a squint.'

'That pretty much describes us,' said Bonney.

'I'd say it does. I was you I wouldn't hang around too long. Only a matter of time before those Indians catch up.'

'Who's gonna tell them where we're at? You?' Bonney's hand had gone to his gunbelt.

'I'd say it's a possibility.'

'You don't seem afraid, Turner,' said Moresby. 'Clay's a fast draw. More'n that, there's four of us. Only two of you.'

'Sometimes in the past that's all we've needed.' Ben told him.

I heard movement to my right. I glanced across and saw O'Donnell rise from behind the bar. He had a Winchester in his hands; it was aimed at Bonney.

'Make that three,' he said, tightening his finger on the trigger. 'You with the scar'll be the first to take a bullet.'

Bonney took his hand from his holster and backed up to the door.

'C'mon, fellas,' he said. 'We'll go and see Holden.' He gave Ben a menacing look. 'This business isn't over, Turner, just postponed. We'll settle it next time.'

CHAPTER NINE

'The countryside out here is absolutely beautiful, don't you think, Wes?' said Abby. We were sitting on a blanket in the shade of a cottonwood tree and had just finished eating. I'd brought Tommy a small fishing net from the store and he was standing beside a stream nearby, trawling for fish.

'Sure is, Abby.' I called to her son. 'Caught anything yet, Tommy?'

'No big fishes, Wes,' he replied. 'Just teeny ones.'

'They're minnows, Tommy. If it's OK with your mom, you can put them in the jar and take them home.'

'Can I, Mommy?'

'Of course, darling. Just don't go too near the water.'

Tommy half-filled the jar I'd given him with

water, upended the net, then shook out the minnows.

'Do you prefer here to Baltimore, Abby?' I asked. 'I can't imagine what it would be like to live in a city.'

'I much prefer it, Wes. Oh, there are some things I miss. Theatres, libraries, that sort of thing. I don't miss the crowds, though. You can breathe easier out here. I'm sure you'd find the city restrictive.'

'You could be right, Abby. I've spent most of my life in the country.'

'Where are you from? I mean originally.'

'My folks were from Jackson, Michigan. They moved to Nebraska when I was two. I was brought up in a little town called Bellevue. My father was a fur trapper. I followed him into the trade, but I didn't like it. Travelled west and worked on a ranch till I was twenty-two. Joined the army a couple of years before the war started.'

'Eliza said you and Ben became prospectors after the war?'

'Yeah. We were kinda restless, I guess. Tried some other things, but never could settle. Then one day we met an old-timer who panned for a living. He showed us the ropes. We worked with him for a couple of years until he died, then we continued on our own. Never made much, but we got by.'

'Well, you seem to have taken to your new profession very well.' Abby smiled. 'All the townsfolk I've talked to say you're very pleasant to deal with.'

'Well, Ben and I have Eliza to thank for helping us get to know the merchandise. But, yeah, I'd say Ben and I are taking to it OK. We weren't sure if we'd be able to when we began.'

Abby's face suddenly took on a worried look.

'Something wrong, Abby?'

'I just remembered about Holden and his men. I'm afraid for you, Wes.'

'Can't say it ain't a problem, Abby. Holden's been threatening to damage the property of merchants who don't pay for protection. Ben and I won't give in to his demands.'

'I really can't blame either of you for feeling that way. But if you confront him on your own you risk getting hurt. Can't the other merchants stand with you?'

'Ben and I were discussing that. We're going to bring it up with them.'

Tommy ran over and held up his jar.

'See, Wes, I've got a whole jarful of minnis.'

'Minnows, Tommy,' Abby corrected him. 'They're lovely, aren't they?'

'Yes, Mommy, they are. Will they grow into big

fishes?' Then Tommy yawned.

'I think some of them will, Tommy. We'll have to wait and see, won't we?' She pushed his hair back from his face. 'I think you're tired, darling. Time we were getting home.'

I took my watch from my vest pocket.

'Sorry Abby, it's twenty after six. I didn't mean to keep you out so late.'

'Nonsense, Wes. I put Tommy to bed around seven. The drive back won't take us long.'

Tommy was asleep when we got back and I took him down from the buggy.

'Would you mind carrying him through, Wes?' Abby asked 'His room's next to the kitchen.'

I put Tommy to bed. Abby followed me through and drew a cover over him.

'Thanks, Wes,' she said. 'I'll change him into his pyjamas in a minute. Would you like a coffee before you go?'

'Much appreciated, but no thanks, I'd better get back. I told Ben I'd be back by half past seven. He's taking Eliza to Mason's for dinner. It's better if one of us is there to mind the store.'

Abby walked me to the door and smiled.

'You know, I think Eliza's fallen for Ben.'

'Yes, I think she has. I'm sure he's sweet on her, too.'

She stood on tiptoe and put her arms round my neck.

'I feel the same about you as Eliza does about Ben,' she said softly. 'You know that, don't you, Wes?'

I pulled her close and kissed her. We held the embrace for a long moment, then I stood back and looked in her eyes.

'I got deep feelings for you, too, Abby.'

Abby smiled, then glanced to the gate. Her blissful look changed to one of shock.

I wheeled around and saw a red-bearded man leaning on the fence post. He smiled at us.

'Quite a touching scene,' he said.

Abby gave a low moan and passed out. I caught her, took her back into the house, then sat her down on a chair. The man followed me inside and stood at my back. He was aged around thirty, and had a fleshy look to him.

'Who the hell are you?' I demanded. 'What do you want?'

'Maybe it's me who should be asking you that question, mister,' he replied. 'That's my wife you were canoodling with. My name's Luke Doherty. I'm Abby's husband.'

Abby gave a soft moan and came to.

'Luke,' she said. 'Luke . . . it can't be. You died

five years ago.'

'Sorry, I didn't mean to alarm you, Abby. But I ain't dead, as you can plainly see.'

'I thought I recognized your stance.' Abby fixed her gaze on him. 'I don't understand. Mr McClure told me you'd been killed in a stampede.'

'It's my fault, Abby,' he said. 'I didn't mean to distress you, either then or now. But I had to make you believe I was dead. It was either that or I'd've died for real.'

'You *had* to? What exactly do you mean?'

'I got Ned McClure to tell you I'd been killed – for a very good reason.'

'What possible reason could you have to make me believe you were dead?' Abby's face had regained its colour, now her cheeks were reddening in anger.

'I'm sorry, Abby,' said Doherty. 'Please, I'd like to explain.'

Abby gave him a searching look but said nothing.

'I staged my death because I'd got into trouble in Abilene. We had a three-day stopover there every time we delivered cattle to the railheads. I sat in on a poker game at the Diamond saloon on my first trip and won some money. Then the next time I went I lost those winnings, plus that month's wages. The owner, Ernie Tucker, gave me a line of credit:

two hundred dollars, so I kept on gambling.'

'How could you possibly take that risk?' Abby asked.

'Well, I won it back to begin with. Even cleared a little profit.' Doherty shifted on his feet. 'Anyway, I got into the habit of gambling every time I reached town. Before long I was in over my head. I reached my limit and went beyond it. Hit a losing streak and ended up owing Tucker more than six hundred dollars.

'Eventually I realized there was no way I could pay it back. I started avoiding the Diamond when we got into town. Next thing I knew Tucker had gunmen out looking for me. He spoke to the ramrod of another outfit from our ranch, Jim Rooney. Told him to tell me I'd pay in dollars or pay in blood. Said it'd be a warning to others.'

'Surely he wouldn't have carried out his threat?' Abby looked shocked.

' 'Course he would've. You don't cross men like Tucker and expect to get away with it. He meant it, Abby. He absolutely convinced Jim Rooney.'

'You could have gone to the marshal in Abilene. Told him a threat had been made to your life.'

'No real law in Abilene, Abby. Anyway, Tucker's enforcers would've shot me 'fore I'd a chance to. They'd've said I'd pulled a pistol on them.'

'Why not come home? We could have left Copper Creek.'

'Don't you see they'd have easily caught up, Abby? Then you really would have been a widow.'

'I've spent the last five years believing I was one.'

'I always planned on coming back. Faked my death to give me a little time till the heat was off.'

'Five years is more than a little time.'

'I had to be sure. I was on another drive to Kansas, ramrodded by Jack Henderson, when old Billy White, our cook, took a fever and died. We buried him near Amarillo. A day later we crossed paths with Jim Rooney, who told me then about Tucker's threat. I explained to Henderson and he advised me to hightail it.

'Told me if he ran into Tucker's men he'd say I'd been killed in a stampede. Said he'd give them the location of Billy's grave if they asked where I was buried. I got Ned McClure to tell you I'd been killed in case Tucker or his men came to Copper Creek. Ned really didn't want to, but I said I'd tell you the truth when I could.'

'Which has taken you all of five years,' Abby said sarcastically.

'Like I mentioned, I had to be sure Tucker thought I was dead. I lay low for a while in Indian Territory. Put on some weight and grew me this

beard. Got by for a while as a muleskinner. Came
back to Texas after six months and joined another
outfit herding longhorns to Wichita along the
Chisholm Trail.'

Doherty gave Abby a beseeching look.

'I know what I done was a hurtful thing, Abby,
and you've every right to be mad. It took me a while
to mend my ways, but I have. I spent the last three
years saving so's I'd have money to come back with.'
He reached into his shirt and took out a leather
wallet. 'Got me five hundred dollars. It's yours and
the boy's, Abby. Won't you forgive me? Can't we
make a new start?'

Abby's eyes took on a steely look.

'I don't want your money, Luke,' she said. 'And I
don't want you, either. You left me almost penniless.
If it hadn't been for the kindness of the people in
Copper Creek Tommy and I wouldn't have survived. What you did was unforgivable. There's
nothing between us now. I want you to leave.'

Doherty straightened up and put the wallet back.

'I see.' He looked at me then back at Abby. 'A
new man in your life, that it? Saw you two were
friendly when I came to the gate.' He nodded in the
direction of Tommy's room. 'Thing is, the boy's
mine, ain't he? You can't stop me seeing him.'

'You've never been near him in five years and you

think all you've to do is turn up and demand to see him now?'

'I ain't demandin', Abby, I'm asking.' Doherty pleaded.

'Tommy's asleep,' said Abby. 'I'm not going to disturb him. Please, I want you out of this house.'

'I'm his father, Abby. I got rights. I'm sure there's a lawyer in this town who would agree.' Doherty patted the wallet in his shirt. 'I'm gonna have a word with him. You ain't gonna stop me seein' my son.'

Abby bristled with anger.

'You're not the only one who can see a lawyer,' she said. She pointed to the door. 'Now get out of my house.'

Doherty stared at Abby in stunned surprise, but he didn't move.

'You heard the lady, mister,' I said, nodding to the door. 'Be on your way.'

Doherty looked at me and shook his head dismissively.

'Don't worry, I'm going. But neither of you has heard the last of me.'

He went out of the door and I followed to make sure he'd gone.

'You OK, Abby?' I asked.

'I am, Wes,' she replied. 'I was shocked and

angry, but I feel better now. Thanks for staying with me.'

'That's OK, Abby. I'd better get back to the store. Let me know if he comes back.'

'Thanks, Wes. But I don't think I'll see him again tonight.'

CHAPTER TEN

'You don't honestly think there's a chance she'll take him back?' said Ben.

We were at the store at noon next day, moving sacks on to the boardwalk for a customer who'd gone to pick up his rig at Sweet's stable.

I hoisted the sack I was carrying on to the pile already there. I'd told Ben what had happened the night before, and gave voice to my misgivings.

'She told him it was over, but you can never be sure.'

'But you said she mentioned her feelings for you before Doherty showed up.'

'Exactly. *Before* Doherty showed up.'

'For Chris'sake, Wes! The man's been out of her life for five years.'

'He's still Tommy's father.'

'That'd count in most circumstances, Wes, but the fella's been gone all that time. You said he got a drover to tell her he'd been killed. Left her to fend for herself and the unborn boy?'

'Yeah, he did.'

'Pretty damnable if you ask me. Man's gotta be low to put his family through that to save his own skin. Don't see he's got the right to call himself a father.'

'You're right, Ben. Don't suppose he has.'

'Can't see Abby changing her mind. She'll most likely divorce him.'

As Ben placed the last sack on the pile three men crossed street and stopped beside the store. The man in front had a dignified look to him and walked with a stick. He tipped his hat.

'Afternoon, Ben. I was wondering if we could have a word.'

Ben looked up.

'Afternoon, Mr Mason. Sure, what can I do for you?'

Mason waved his stick in the direction of the men behind him.

'This is Horace Appleby, owner of the furniture emporium, and this is Daniel Gorman, town carpenter and undertaker.' He cleared his throat. 'It's about Ed Holden and his men.' Then he nodded towards me. 'I'm sorry, Ben, I haven't met your partner.'

'This is Wes Noble,' Ben said. 'Wes, this is Mr Mason, owner of the restaurant over on the next block.'

'The one with the stereopticon show?' I asked.

'Yes, Mr Noble, that's correct,' Mason said. 'I've a new feature in the back room every other week.'

'Pleased to meet you, Mr Mason.'

'Call me Ches, please.'

Ben thumbed to the door. 'Why don't the three of you come in out of the sun?'

Mason stepped on to the boardwalk followed by Appleby and Gorman.

'Thank you, Ben, much appreciated,' said Mason.

The three took off their hats and came into the store. Mason addressed Ben.

'I'll get straight to the point. It's about Holden and his so-called protection. All the merchants had a visit from his two cohorts this morning.'

'Burnett and McKenna?'

'Yes. The thing is, Ben, Holden's upped his weekly charges from fifty dollars to seventy-five.'

'McKenna told us it was on account of you refusing to pay,' Appleby added, running a finger under his collar. 'Said he was putting a penalty on each of the other merchants.'

Appleby was tall, reedy-looking, and sported an imperial-style moustache. Mason held up a hand.

'Please, Horace. Holden's only using that as an excuse to extort more money.'

'I'm already paying more than I can afford,' Gorman said. He was the smallest of the trio, and blinked rapidly as he spoke.

'Then why pay it?' asked Ben.

Gorman scratched his head but said nothing.

'There's only one way to stop Holden,' Ben said. 'Everyone in Copper Creek has to stand together. Face up to him.'

'Well, we were going to ask your advice on how to deal with it,' Mason said. 'But I'm not sure about gunplay.'

'Is there any other way to deal with it?'

'None of us are particularly brave men, Ben. And not all of us are used to firearms.'

'I understand that,' said Ben. 'That's what Holden's counting on. But don't you think that if enough merchants and townsfolk were willing to make a stand Holden would lose his power to intimidate?'

'What do you suggest, Ben?' Mason asked.

'The three of you have a word with the town's other merchants. Citizens, too. Talk to Nick Carter. Arrange a meeting for seven o'clock tonight. Say it's to discuss how we can work together to stop Holden. Wes and I will be there.'

That evening I counted more than forty men in the back room of the Alamo. Carter had set up chairs in rows and cleared the room of tables. All the merchants were there, but I guessed they made up just a quarter of those present. The remainder were Copper Creek citizens and ranchers from the surrounding area.

Ben and I arrived just after seven and Mason seated us next to him. Once everyone was in place Mason stood up and addressed the assembly.

'I asked you all here to talk about the problems with Holden and his gang. You're all aware that since he bought the Miller place he's ridden roughshod over the town.

'What those of you here who aren't merchants may not know is that Holden's been extorting money from the town's businesses, my own included. Each of us has been threatened with arson if we refuse.

'Now, some of you may think this doesn't affect you, but it does. Most of us have been forced to put a penny or two on everything we sell in order to get by.'

The was a low murmur, then some among the

gathering began to voice indignation.

'. . . damn Holden. . . .'

'. . . shouldn't be allowed to get away with it. . . .'

'. . . time something was done about him and his hired gunslingers. . . .'

'. . . let 'em go elsewhere. . . .'

'. . . bunch of thievin' varmints. . . .'

'Please, gentlemen,' Mason put up a hand. 'We're here to discuss a solution. Ben Turner and Wes Noble took over the general store when Arthur Grace retired two weeks ago. They were also approached by Holden's men and asked to pay. They refused, and sent Holden's thugs away with a boot up their backsides. They've not been disturbed since. They're here to advise us on how we might make a stand.' He turned and waved a hand in Ben's direction. 'If you please, Mr Turner.' He sat down. Ben rose to his feet.

'First off, I'd like to say that Wes and I have met Holden and his men,' he said. 'They paid us a visit at the Alamo when we first came to town. There were eleven of them then, including Holden. He's since been joined by four more. Fifteen in all.'

A wiry-looking man in his sixties stood up. He took a pipe from his mouth and pointed the stem at Ben.

'All of 'em hired killers, don't forget,' he said.

'That's right,' Ben replied. 'All of them carry guns and know how to use them. But when it comes down to it they're men, same's you and me. None of them's invincible.'

'Ben braced two of them outside this saloon when we first arrived,' I said. 'One had a fast draw and went for his pistols. Ben outshot him. The other man backed down.'

'What we're saying is: Holden and those with him are bullies,' continued Ben. 'Stand up to them and they'll crack.'

Horace Appleby was sitting near the back. He stood up.

'That's easy for you to say, Mr Turner. You're ex-military.'

'I am, but don't see as that makes a difference. Anyone here not know how to use a rifle?'

No one made a response.

'Fine,' said Ben. 'Anyone been in the army?'

A freckle-faced man in his twenties put his hand up.

'I served with the Second Texas Infantry,' he said. 'Got me a sharpshooter medal.'

'Good,' Ben said. 'What's your name, friend?'

'Task, Mr Turner. Billy Task.'

'OK, Billy. Will you stand with us?'

'Sure I will, Mr Turner.'

'Anyone else?' asked Ben.

'I know how to handle a rifle, Ben.'

I looked to my right and saw Nick Carter's barman standing at the entrance.

'Mr O'Donnell,' Ben said. 'Of course. Sorry – I never got around to thanking you properly for helping us see off the Bonney twins.'

' 'Twas a pleasure, Ben. Me name's Liam, by the way.'

'Thanks, Liam. That makes Billy, Liam, Wes and me. Anyone else?'

CHAPTER ELEVEN

Ten minutes later twenty-three of the men in the room had volunteered. We arranged to rendezvous at the Alamo next time Holden came to town. It was agreed that Ben would assign each of us a vantage point and we'd await his signal before shooting.

One of the last to come forward was Stanley Coleman, a grocer whose premises were at the top end of Main Street. Coleman told us Holden's men had recently begun to collect groceries at his store on a Saturday.

'They came to me soon after you took over old man Grace's place,' he said. 'Fella called Toby and another man called Dunstan came in as usual a week ago and I paid them their fifty bucks. Then they called again the next day, Saturday. Told me to make up a grocery order. I asked them why they

weren't getting their supplies at Grace's as they nor-
mally did. Told me to mind my own business.'

Ben looked at me. 'Must've been the day after we
saw off Burnett and McKenna.'

I nodded agreement. 'They due to call in tomorrow?' I asked Coleman.

'Yeah,' he replied. 'Around noon, most likely.'

'Good,' Ben said. 'Time to poke a stick into the
hornet's nest. Wes and I will be there to meet them.
Make sure they go away empty handed. That'll
bring this thing to a head – force Holden's hand.'

After we closed the store that night I went back to
Abby's house. I thought Doherty could pay her
another visit, and I was concerned that he might
threaten her.

Of course that wasn't the only reason. Even
though Ben thought she'd be unlikely to take
Doherty back, I wasn't so sure. I realized my feelings
for her ran deep, and hoped Doherty's return
hadn't changed the way she felt about me.

It was growing dark when I knocked her door. I
saw a light in the parlour and knew she was home.
Even so, I had to knock a second time before Abby
answered. When she came to the door she
appeared anxious.

'Oh, it's you, Wes,' she said. 'Please, come in.'

'Evening, Abby. You look worried. Luke been bothering you?'

'No,' she said, then hesitated. 'Well, not exactly.'

'He came by again?'

'Yes, this afternoon. He was apologetic and appeared sincere. Says he can imagine my shock after thinking myself a widow all this time. Went on to admit what he did was selfish, but told me he'd changed his ways. He asked me to take him back, at least for Tommy's sake. Says he'll get back his old job at the mine.'

'You trust him, Abby? After what he put you through?'

'I'm so terribly confused.' A tear ran down her cheek, she took my hand. 'Wes, please believe I meant what I said about my feelings for you. It's just . . .'

'It's Tommy, isn't it?'

'Yes, Wes, it is. I'm worried I might be putting myself first. Luke's right; he's Tommy's father. If I exclude him now, banish him from my son's life, Tommy might resent that later.'

'Did Luke see Tommy today?'

'Yes, I let him stay an hour. He played with him for a while.'

'Does the boy know who he is?'

'No, Wes. He's too young to understand. I made

Luke promise he wouldn't mention it for now.'

'So you'll take Luke back for Tommy's sake?'

She dabbed a handkerchief to her eyes.

'I don't know, Wes, I honestly don't know. Everything's happened so suddenly. I only want what's best for my son.'

'You know what they say about history repeating itself, Abby? Take him back and there's a fair chance he'll move on. Leave you high and dry a second time.'

'I understand that, Wes. I've thought about it a lot these past hours. I'm not that naive. I know Luke's character from old, believe me.'

'But it comes back to Tommy?'

'Yes, Wes, I'm afraid it does.'

'You know I'd be happy to marry you, Abby. I wouldn't be Tommy's blood father but I'd raise him as my own.'

'Before Luke came back, Wes, I'd have accepted without a second's hesitation.'

'You could divorce him.'

'I know, Wes. I may do that but, honestly, I need time to think it over.'

'OK, Abby. When will you decide?'

'I told Luke I'd give him an answer in a couple of days. Please understand, Wes, whatever happens doesn't change the way I feel about you. I'm only thinking about Tommy.'

'I take it Luke's staying in town?'

'Yes, he's staying at a boarding house at the south end of Main Street.'

'Ma Porter's place?'

'Yes, that's right.'

'You'll let me know, Abby?'

'I promise, Wes.' She kissed me. 'I'll give Luke his answer by Sunday evening. I'll let you know before then.'

I walked along Main Street and arrived at Ma Porter's boarding house a few minutes later. The place had cream-coloured paint flaking from the timber and looked a bit shabby. I stepped on to the porch and knocked on the door. It was answered by short, dumpy woman who had her hair tied in a bun.

'Sorry, mister,' she said. 'All my rooms are taken.'

'It's OK, ma'am. I'm not looking for a room. You Mrs Porter?'

'Yes, I am.'

'I believe you've a man called Luke Doherty staying with you. I was wondering if I might have a word with him.'

'Yes, I think he's here. Wait a minute and I'll get him.'

She went inside, leaving the door just ajar. Moments later I heard her knock on a door on the upper landing, then came muffled voices, followed by the tramping of boots on the stairs.

The door opened again and Doherty stood there.

'You wanted something?'

'Yeah. Can we talk for a minute?'

Doherty came out on to the boardwalk and closed the door behind him. He took a freshly rolled cigarette from behind his ear, lit it, then drew in the smoke and exhaled.

'Sure,' he said. 'What do you want?'

'It's about Abby.'

'You talk to her?'

'Yeah, matter of fact I did.'

He gave me a look of curiosity. 'She tell you she might take me back?'

'Said she was giving it consideration.'

'Thing is, Mr Noble . . .' he paused, 'Noble *is* your name, ain't it?'

'Uh-huh.'

'Thing is, Mr Noble, Abby's got the boy to consider. I explained Tommy's interests would be best served if his father was around. Think she's beginning to realize that.'

'The way his father's been looking after his interests so far, you mean?'

Doherty scowled. 'No need for sarcasm, Noble. I already explained why that was.'

'Yeah, you did. How much did you make in your six months as a muleskinner?'

'Five hundred or so, why?'

'Just curious. And how much did you make a month as a drover working the Chisholm?'

'Forty bucks a month. Not that it's anything to do with you.'

'Heard what you offered Abby when you spoke to her yesterday. Five hundred don't seem a lot to put by in five years, does it? Given what you were making.'

'Watcha mean?'

'You're still gambling, aren't you, Luke?'

'Like I told Abby, I've changed my ways.'

'Mean to tell me you haven't been in a poker game recently?'

'Not for more'n a year.'

'Know what I think, Luke?'

'What?' Doherty shrugged nonchalantly.

'You're still gambling,' I said. 'I think you had a sizeable win lately. Somewhere in southern Texas. San Antonio or El Paso, maybe. For the first time in years you've got more than a few dollars in your pocket. Probably just ended a drive and felt no pressing need to go on another one.

'So you got to wondering what your son looked like. Decided to come and have a look-see. Then you discovered Abby hadn't remarried and thought you might persuade her to give you another chance. Of course if she does, you'll be happy to take on the role of husband and father again. That is, until the urge to gamble overcomes the need to live up to your responsibilities.'

'I came to see my boy,' Doherty said. 'Nothing wrong with that, is there? And if Abby'll have me there's nothing wrong with that either.'

'Even if it means stretching the truth?'

'So what if I've had the odd game? I'm ahead, ain't I? That's all that matters.'

'All that matters to you. But it's not what's important to Abby or Tommy.'

'Duck out, Noble. Ain't none of your business.'

'Ain't it?' I felt anger rising within me and I grabbed him by the shirt. 'I'm gonna make you a promise, Doherty. Hurt either one of them – in any way – and I'll make it my business.'

CHAPTER TWELVE

The next day Ben and I were waiting in the back room of Coleman's store when Toby and Dunstan arrived. Toby looked as dishevelled as he'd been when we first saw him with Lester Green. Dunstan, his new crony, was older and thicker round the waist, but every bit as grubby. We watched from behind a bead curtain as the two of them walked up to the counter.

'Groceries for the ranch,' Dunstan said to Coleman. 'Got 'em made up yet?'

Coleman shuffled his feet and looked a bit uncomfortable.

'Ah, yes, Mr Holden's order,' he said. 'Ahem, there's been a bit of difficulty.'

'Difficulty?' said Dunstan. 'What difficulty?'

Ben pulled back the curtain and went into the front of the store with me at his back.

'Difficulty with delivery,' he said. 'On account of Mr Holden being banned from Copper Creek, together with anyone who works for him. You boys'll need to get your supplies elsewhere.'

Dunstan wheeled round in surprise and his hand went to his side. Toby blanched when he saw Ben and backed to the door. Dunstan saw his companion withdraw, but didn't flinch; his hand remained poised over his gunbelt.

'Who says?'

'Copper Creek Citizens Committee. Newly formed with new rules.' Ben stepped a pace nearer. 'We want you to tell Mr Holden there'll be no more need for protection. His services ain't any longer required.'

'We came for our grocery order.' Dunstan stood his ground, scowling. 'Ain't leaving without it.'

'Think you'll have to do just that,' Ben told him. Dunstan turned to Coleman.

'You gonna get us get our order?'

Coleman didn't reply.

'Sounds like you don't understand,' Ben said. 'Neither Mr Coleman nor any other merchant in Copper Creek's gonna do business with you.' He nodded to the door. 'Now, why don't you leave?'

103

Dunstan pivoted on his heels and stood to face Ben.

'What'll you do if we don't?' he said. Toby shook his head as though in warning.

'Don't, Jack,' he said. 'He's the man who shot Lester.'

Dunstan glanced at Toby, then back at Ben.

'I draw a fast pistol, too, mister. Could be you ain't as quick as you think.'

'Could be,' Ben said. 'Only one way to find out.'

The atmosphere was tense for a moment as Dunstan weighed things up. He glanced at Coleman, then glowered at Ben. He shook his head.

'OK. Got it your way for now.' He went to the door. 'Ain't gonna stay that way for long.'

After the men had left the volunteers took it in turns to keep watch. Two men were posted, one at each end of town, with instructions to fire a warning shot if Holden's gang was sighted.

The remainder of Saturday passed without incident, but at nine on Sunday morning Ben and I were finishing breakfast when we heard rifle fire at the south end of town. We made our way to the Alamo, where we were joined by the others.

Liam O'Donnell was one of the first to arrive, followed seconds later by Billy Task.

'Amos Waterman fired,' Billy said. 'He's watching the south road from the roof of Ma Porter's place.'

Waterman came up running.

'Riders coming in from the south,' he said breathlessly. 'Looks like the entire bunch.' Ben got the men to make sure women and children were told to remain indoors, then quickly assigned each man to his vantage point: eight covering the approaches at either end of town and nine others, Ben and me included, to watch the centre.

'It's certain sure Holden'll split his forces,' Ben said. 'Liam, you and your men take the north end. Billy, you and your fellas cover the south. The rest of us'll watch the intersecting streets. Hold your fire till they're in range.'

We dispersed. Ben and I went to the roof of Mason's restaurant, from where we had a clear view of all approaches. I trained my binoculars on the south road and thumbed the focus wheel.

'Fifteen riders coming in fast,' I told Ben.

'I see 'em,' he said. 'Ain't they starting to diverge?'

I refocused the glasses. 'Yeah, they are. They're splitting into three groups. Middle group's staying on the south road. Other two diverting east and west.'

'See Holden?'

'Yeah, I think he's on the south approach.'

Holden and the five with him were only yards from town when the first shot rang out. The shooter was Billy Task, whose round caught the chest of the rider on Holden's left. The man catapulted from his horse and crashed to the ground. Sustained fire forced the other five to dismount and run for cover; one to the rear of a privy, Holden and the two with him to the back of a brick outhouse.

Meanwhile the two other groups had reached town's outskirts. The second group swung east and headed to the north end of town; there they were fired on by Liam's men, who managed to drop one before the remainder reached their objective.

The man killed was McKenna, who'd been with Burnett when Ben ejected him from the store. Burnett and the other two men with him dismounted hurriedly and hid behind a low rise.

The men who rode in on the other side were more successful. They took cover behind a ridge running parallel with the town a hundred yards to the west. The five in this group were Toby, Lenny Black, Claude Moresby and the Bonney twins.

They quickly sighted their rifles and began shooting. Ben and I returned fire, as did Ches Mason and Amos Waterman, who were either side of us. Lionel

106

Sweet and four others were positioned below us at the western end of the blocks intersecting.

Two minutes into the fight I looked to my left and saw the man at the privy make a run for the corner of Main Street. He'd almost reached the halfway point when one of Billy's men shot him. This was enough to persuade Holden and those with him to remain where they were. They ducked out from the corners now and then, but barely got off a shot before heavy fire forced them back.

'Billy's got the south end covered,' said Ben. 'Holden can't move. Liam and those on the roof of the telegraph office have the others pinned at the north. The main threat is the ridge.'

Ben raised his head a fraction and looked through a two-inch gap in a hoarding at the roof's edge. He nodded towards a dried-out arroyo running from the far side of the telegraph office to north end of the ridge.

'If the others gave us cover, you and I could crawl up that wash and outflank them.'

I took my binoculars and focused on the arroyo.

'Looks about three feet deep. They mightn't see us if we held to the left.'

We told Ches and Amos what we intended to do and went down to the street.

'I'll let Billy and Lionel know,' said Ben when we

107

left the Alamo. 'You speak to Liam. Wait for me this side of the Western Union building.'

I went to the telegraph office and told Liam our plan. Moments later Ben returned; the two of us crouched low and edged to the rear of the building. Once there we sprinted to the arroyo. Liam and his men gave us covering fire, as did the men with Billy and Lionel. Seconds later a continuous volley forced the five on the ridge to keep their heads low.

Burnett, though, had realized that the focus of Liam's fire had shifted. He looked to his right, saw us, and he and two men with him began shooting. I glanced over my shoulder as one of his rounds kicked the earth at my feet.

'It's Burnett and the other two,' I told Ben. 'The entire length of the wash is visible from where they are.'

Ben looked back as another bullet found our range and ricocheted off a nearby stone.

'It'll be better if Liam keeps firing on the ridge,' he said. 'We'll have to deal with Burnett ourselves.'

We scrambled to face this new threat while staying close to the bottom of the ditch. Even so, we were completely exposed from Burnett's position. Burnett quickly took advantage and rolled level with us, just fifty feet distant.

He raised himself on to his elbows and aimed

along the wash. He had Ben in his sights as I brought up my Henry. I fired a fraction ahead of him and his bullet flew wide as my round found its mark. It caught Burnett in the head; he crumpled to the ground.

Meanwhile his two sidekicks were determined to make the most of our vulnerability. They began shooting from a standing position, but were spotted by one of Liam's men on the Western Union roof. He swung round and fired; his round felled the shooter nearest us. He fired again. His second shot smashed into the remaining man's chest.

Ben and I resumed our crawl up the arroyo while the volunteers fired on the ridge. We reached a point level with the north end, and saw that Clem Bonney and Lenny Black were the nearest shooters.

'We got a clear field of fire to those two,' I said. 'Toby, Clay Bonney and Moresby are further up.'

But Clem Bonney and Black had crouched low and were difficult to target. Every now and then, however, there was a lull in the shooting and they rose to fire.

'Next time they show their heads, Wes, you target Black,' Ben said. 'I'll take Bonney.'

The firing from the end of town nearest us ceased suddenly. I looked across and saw Liam wave his Stetson.

'Look, Ben,' I said. 'Liam's stopped shooting. He knows we're after these two.'

Ben glanced at the telegraph office roof.

'You're right,' he said. 'Get ready, Wes. It's likely they'll make a move soon.'

As Ben had predicted Bonney and Black raised their heads a few seconds later.

Ben and I fired. Bonney was in the act of sighting his rifle when Ben's round hit him just above the ear. There was an explosion of blood and Bonney's head jerked back. Almost simultaneously my shot hit Black in the left side of his chest; he lolled to his right, twitched for a moment, then lay still.

Ben and I left the arroyo then and headed towards the other shooters. We'd only covered a third of the way, however, when we heard the drumming of hoofs and saw the volunteers redirect their fire.

Moments later we gained the high part of the ridge. Below us, Clay Bonney, Moresby and Toby were headed south, all three urging their mounts to a fast gallop.

CHAPTER THIRTEEN

'Holden and the other two must've sneaked out while we were targeting the ridge,' Amos Waterman said. He and the other volunteers, together with Ben and myself, were standing at the front of the Alamo a short while later. Liam and Billy remained on watch in case Holden returned.

'Yeah; saw the way the fight was going and skedaddled,' Lionel Sweet added. Ches Mason nodded his head in agreement.

'Clay Bonney saw you shoot his brother and the other fella, Ben,' he said. 'I saw him and the man with him mount up and vamoose.'

'Was anyone hurt on our side?'

'Abe Wood, the barber, is the only casualty. Took a bullet in the shoulder. I'm sure he'll be fine. I've sent a man to fetch Doc Taylor.'

Ben nodded. 'Then we'd better ask Mr Gorman

to take care of the dead.'

'Dan's got it in hand, Ben,' Mason told him. 'He and his man have taken a wagon. Bringing them in now.'

Ben rubbed his neck. 'Thanks, Ches.'

'Do you think it's all up with Holden?'

'No, I don't. There's still seven men left, every one of them a threat to the town. Only way to get peace is to finish it.'

'You're thinking of going to Holden's place?'

'Can't see how we can end it otherwise.'

We were interrupted by a shout; we turned to see Liam running from the Western Union office. He had a telescope in his hand; he waved it to attract our attention.

'A large group of riders north of the town,' he said when he reached us. 'Saw them from the top of the telegraph office. Look like Indians. Fifty, maybe sixty.'

Ben and I went to Mason's roof where I sighted my glasses.

'There's a mess of Indians a mile out,' I said.

'Can you see how many?' asked Ben.

I calibrated the wheel to improve the focus.

'At least sixty – maybe more.'

'Apaches?'

I thumbed the wheel again and brought the

front riders into focus.

'Yeah. It's the Mescaleros we met near Twin Buttes. Lone Wolf and Grey Owl. You were right, Ben. They've gotten others to ride with them.'

'Dime'll get you a dollar they found the Bonney twins' tracks. Followed them here to Copper Creek.'

'But Clem Bonney and Lenny Black are dead. The other two are with Holden.'

'Lone Wolf don't know that,' said Ben. I trained the glasses on the Apaches again.

'They've reined in their horses. Don't know why, but they've stopped.'

'Making plans to attack.' Ben went to the stairs. 'Come on, Wes. The town's in danger. We've got to stop them.'

'*Stop* them, Ben? How can we? There's only you, me and twenty-three volunteers. We'd be massacred.'

'If we tried to take them on, yes, we would. Don't plan on doing that. Only reason Lone Wolf's here is 'cause he's after the Bonneys and their henchmen. OK, so two of them're dead. We gotta prove it. Let him know where he can get his hands on Clay and Moresby.'

We got back to the street and saw anxiety on the volunteers' faces.

113

'Is it true, Ben?' asked Mason. 'There's really a horde of Indians outside the town?'

'There is,' Ben replied. 'But Wes and I think we know why they're here.' He stepped on to the boardwalk. 'Listen everybody. Wes and I ran into these Indians three weeks ago, just before we arrived in Copper Creek.

'There was an incident at a Mescalero camp the other side of Twin Buttes. Three Indian women and two children were fetching water when the Bonneys came along with Moresby and Black. Clay Bonney raped and killed a young squaw, who had her two kids with her. They then shot an older woman, the squaw's mother. When the third squaw got hold of the young 'uns and tried to escape, they shot them, too. Killed the kids; left the woman for dead.'

'Did the Indians try to kill you?' asked Billy.

'No, Billy,' I replied. 'Ben and I were on our way to El Paso. Fifteen of them overcame us and took us to their camp. When the squaw who survived said we weren't involved, they let us go.'

'So what are you planning to do, Ben?' asked Mason.

'The Apaches are here because of Bonney and his cronies,' replied Ben. 'Two of those are dead. Wes and I are gonna prove that, tell them where they can find the others. Has Gorman brought back those dead men?'

'I think his wagon's at the rear of his premises,' Mason said.

'Good. Ches, will you ask him to bring us the bodies of Clay Bonney and Lenny Black?'

'Right away, Ben.' He walked off. Ben addressed Sweet.

'Lionel, have you stabled the dead men's horses?'

'Yeah,' Sweet replied. 'But only the five at the north. Ain't fetched the ones on the ridge yet.'

'OK. Will you bring two of them here?'

'Sure thing, Ben.' Sweet hurried off in the direction of the stable.

Minutes later Ben and I had slung Bonney's and Black's bodies across two horses and were headed out of town. As soon as we had cleared the town limits I studied the plain.

'Don't think Lone Wolf's moved since we looked last,' I said. 'Taking him some time to make up his mind.'

'Likely he's figurin' where our shooters would be placed for defence,' replied Ben. 'If the Indians attack the town they won't stop and look for cover. They'll pour in every which way, targeting any vulnerable entry point.'

'But you might get him to stay his hand?' I

thumbed to the horses trailing us. 'If you tell them these men were with Holden at his ranch?'

'Hope so. Like I say, I'm sure he's here because their tracks lead to Copper Creek. Probably thinks they're holed up in the town. Understandable assumption in the circumstances.'

The Apaches were now just a half-mile from us. We looked across and saw Lone Wolf raise a coup stick.

'I think he's signalling the others to hold their positions,' said Ben. 'Knows we want to talk.'

'Just as well we came without weapons,' I said. Ben smiled weakly.

'Wouldn't've made a whole lot of difference if we'd had 'em, Wes. Given the odds.'

The Apaches were ranked in four columns: around fifteen braves in each. Lone Wolf and Grey Owl were at the centre of the front column. As we approached they gently heeled the flanks of their ponies and moved forward. Ben raised a hand in greeting.

'Grey Owl,' he said. 'Lone Wolf.'

Lone Wolf turned to Grey Owl and spoke.

'My leader want to know why you come to meet us,' Grey Owl interpreted. Ben indicated the bodies tied to the horses behind us.

'We've brought two of the men who killed the

116

wife and children of Lone Wolf's brother. They were shot in a gunfight in Copper Creek.'

Grey Owl pointed to the town.

'Copper Creek is the name of this place?'

'Yes,' Ben replied.

'Who shot these men?'

'The people of Copper Creek. The four who killed the squaws and children near your camp were hired gunslingers. They were working for a man called Holden, who's been strong-arming the town's merchants. This man threatened to damage their properties unless he was given money. The people stopped paying and he attacked the town. These men were shot in the gunfight.'

'What about man with scar and one with squint eye?' Grey Owl asked.

'They attacked the town with the man called Holden. Both of them got away.'

'Why you also in the town? I thought you work rivers for yellow dust.'

'We did, but we used the gold we had to buy a store in the town. We're against Holden and the killers who work for him.'

'When was this fight?'

'Only this morning. Just before you arrived.'

Lone Wolf listened while Grey Owl translated this exchange, then he walked his pony beyond us and

117

stopped at the horses carrying Bonney and Black. He lifted the head of each by the hair and scrutinized the faces; then he turned his pony and came back.

Lone Wolf spoke again.

'He ask how many with this Holden are alive after battle?' Grey Owl said.

'Seven,' Ben replied.

'They include man with scar and man who have squint?'

'Yes. As I told you, they rode away with Holden. They're back at his ranch now, most likely. We were about to go after him when you showed up.'

'They not in town?'

'No, like I say, they rode off.'

'Where this Holden have ranch?'

'Three miles south-west of town.'

Grey Owl translated and again the Apache leader spoke, this time at length.

'Lone Wolf say you came to our camp and White Bear think you honest men who speak the truth,' Grey Owl told us. 'And that is why we let you go. But he also say to tell you that too many times treaties have been made with the bluecoats, and too many times the same treaties have been broken.

'Now Lone Wolf say he has had enough of the white man's word. You say man with scar and man

118

with squint are with this Holden at ranch south of town. Lone Wolf say he think if we go to this place we not find these men. Maybe they still in town.'

'Why would I lie to you, Grey Owl?' asked Ben.

'Lone Wolf say they could hide in town. Thinks maybe these men have hostage; send you here to throw us off trail. We go to place you say; they escape.'

'Neither of them is in the town, Grey Owl. I give you my word.'

'Lone Wolf no longer take white man's word. He says best way is to surround and attack town. Search every place, shoot anyone who stands in our way. We find these men and kill them.'

'I understand why Lone Wolf finds it hard to trust us. And he's every right to be angry about what happened to his brother's wife and family. But believe me, these men *are* with Holden. Tell Lone Wolf he can stay here and keep watch on the town and make sure nobody leaves. Wes and I will go to Holden's ranch and bring Bonney and Moresby to you.'

'You mean this? Two of you will take on seven men? You understand – if Lone Owl agrees to this he will not let anyone ride with you.'

'I understand,' said Ben. 'Wes and I will go our-selves. We'll ride south and bypass the town. Please,

119

ask him to let us prove we speak the truth.'

Grey Owl translated and Lone Wolf listened. He spoke again; as he did so he made a curving movement with his arm and pointed to the sun.

'Lone Wolf say he agree,' said Grey Owl. 'But he say you have only until the sun touch the earth. We surround town. If you do not bring these men back by then, we attack.'

CHAPTER FOURTEEN

'Pity there wasn't a way we could have gotten word to the others,' I said. 'The townsfolk must think they're likely to be attacked any minute.'

We'd ridden wide of Copper Creek a short while after leaving the Apaches and were back on the south road. The Apaches had shadowed us as far as Copper Creek, where they'd split into two groups and surrounded the town.

'Mason and the others will have been watching us,' Ben said. 'No doubt they saw us ride ahead of the Apaches and make our way south. Likely they'll figure what we're up to.'

'You don't think any of the volunteers'll panic? Start shooting and hasten an attack?'

'It's possible but unlikely. For one thing we saw Lone Wolf's men take up positions half a mile out. Mason's bound to realize there's no imminent threat. He'll have posted the men to their vantage points, of course. But I don't think they'll be shooting if the Indians remain where they are.'

The sun was now almost at its zenith. We reckoned we'd arrive at Holden's place a little after noon, which gave us five hours till sundown. There was a fork in the road near some shinnery oaks, and here we followed a draw to the right. This took us to a series of bluffs, after which the trail twisted and turned for a mile, then led to an open valley. We caught a glimpse of Holden's ranch at the southwest end of the valley floor. We reined in beside a stand of cottonwoods.

Low hills surrounded the valley like a horseshoe. The bow end lay just behind Holden's property, which consisted of a stone-built Spanish-style *hacienda*, with a wooden bunkhouse that stood at right angles to the main dwelling. A large corral with fifty head of horses stood immediately to the right of the bunkhouse.

'We'll circle down the other side of the ridge on the left,' Ben said. 'Climb over the hill and come in behind them. Most likely Holden's expecting a posse, which he'll assume will attack frontally.

They'll be concentrating their watch with that in mind.'

I took my glasses and studied the area around and above the ranch.

'Where do you think they're positioned? I don't see 'em.'

'I'd guess two of them are placed near the house. Most likely in the hills behind it. Higher ground would give them clear sight of any approach. The others could be at the ranch house. If that's the case it might work to our advantage. If we're lucky the shooters on the hill might be Bonney and Moresby.'

'It looks deserted, Ben. Ain't it possible he's high-tailed it?'

'Don't think that's likely.' He pointed to the corral. 'Don't forget these animals. Prime horse-flesh – got to be a few thousand dollars' worth. Can't see him leaving without them. No, he's there and he's waiting. We both know it's easier to defend a position than attack it.'

'Reckon you're right. But it's strange not seeing anyone about.'

'They're there, Wes. Take my word for it.'

We moved off at a gentle canter and swung east around the hills, taking the precaution of using as much natural cover as we could in case someone had been posted to watch.

The brush on that side of the hills was a mixture of mesquite, chaparral and dogwood. Most of this gave reasonable cover, but we had to pick our way carefully in case one of the horses stepped in a gopher hole or stumbled on an exposed root.

Soon we reached the bow end of the hills, where we dismounted at a piñon tree and tethered our mounts. Ben looked to a thumb of rock that stood clear of the ridge at the top.

'Reckon the spur of that bluff is the other side of Holden's ranch house.'

'Think you're right. I remember seeing it with the glasses.'

'OK, let's go. Looks about a hundred feet to the top. Better take our time. Still a chance someone's watching.'

We made our way up the slope, taking care not to disturb any scree and start a rockfall, which might draw attention. The hill was fairly steep until the halfway point, where the rise became more gradual.

Ben and I gained the ridge minutes later. We were only feet away from the bluff when we heard a rifle being levered.

'Hold it right there,' a voice said. 'Either of you moves I'll shoot.'

We looked to the bluff and saw Toby standing

clear of a cleft where he'd been hiding, watching our approach.

'Toby!' said Ben. 'Congratulations; you took us by surprise.'

'I ain't kidding, Turner,' Toby said. 'Another move and I'll pull this trigger.'

Ben and I now stood three feet apart, both of us with our rifles at our sides.

'On your own up here, Toby?' asked Ben. 'Holden didn't think there'd be much chance of anyone coming from behind, did he? That's why he posted only one man.'

Toby's eyes shifted from side to side.

'Bonney and Moresby are on a hill just below me,' he said nervously. 'All I have to do is shout and they'll come up.'

'Don't think they'd get here in time,' Ben said. 'Wes and I ain't standing close enough for you to get off two shots and make your aim count. You shoot me 'n' Wes'll plug you for sure. Vice versa if you try to shoot him.'

Toby shook his head.

'I'll fire. I promise I will.'

'Ain't easy pulling a trigger on a man, is it, Toby? 'Specially close up,' said Ben. He nodded to the rifle. 'Why don't you put the gun down? Wes and I won't shoot you.'

There was a long moment of quiet. Toby was shaking visibly, sweat streaming down his face.

A sudden beating of wings broke the silence as an eagle rose from the other side of the bluff. The unexpected distraction startled Toby. He turned and this gave Ben enough time. He dropped his Spencer, ran over and wrenched the rifle from Toby's grasp, then dug an elbow into the man's gut.

The pole-axed Toby slumped to the ground. Ben took a hold of him and pulled him to the bluff. He propped him up and took his belt, then bound his arms at the back. Toby revived a moment later and Ben pulled him upright.

'Now, Toby,' he said, 'you're gonna walk ahead and show us where Bonney and Moresby are at. Any sound and your jaw'll feel the butt of this Spencer. Understood?'

'Yeah,' Toby replied sullenly.

We followed him along the ridge and came to a trail that wound through trees on the ranch side of the ridge. The trail came up over the hill and continued down the side we'd just climbed, joining the plateau near where we'd tethered our horses.

'Bonney and Moresby came up on horseback?' Ben asked.

'Yeah, we all did. My mount's with theirs.'

'And where are they?'

'At a clearing halfway down, just a little way into the trees. The horses are tethered near by.'

'Holden's at the ranch house?'

'Yeah, him, Jack Dunstan and two Mexicans.'

'OK,' said Ben. He took Toby to a flat rock at the edge of the ridge, then sat him down. He removed the man's bandanna, tied it round his eyes, and turned him so his legs dangled over the side.

'This is so you'll stay put, Toby,' Ben told him. 'There's a hundred foot drop either side of you, so I wouldn't advise getting antsy and moving around. You're liable to break your neck if you do.' Ben took off his own bandanna. 'I'm going to gag you now so you don't call out. I'll remove it and the blindfold when we get back.'

We left the immobilized Toby and moved slowly down the trail, which snaked through a stand of timber and came out just above a grassy promontory. Ben and I took cover at the outer edge of the trees and saw a rocky ledge at the foot of the hill. At its rim were two large boulders, where Bonney and Moresby were hunkered with their rifles held ready. Three horses were tied to some greasewood at the outermost corner. Beyond the ledge Holden's ranch house was clearly visible in the valley beneath.

'I can see why they picked this spot,' Ben said

quietly. 'Straight field of fire up the valley. With this vantage point and the ranch house, they've got a frontal attack pretty well covered.'

I nodded towards Bonney and Moresby.

'Think we can make our move without those two hearing us?'

'With luck, Wes. We'll stay in the trees till we're above their position, then move down. The embankment's grassy from there. If we take our time we should be behind them before they know we're here.'

We inched along the edge of the trees to a spot just above the two men, then crept down slowly with our rifles aimed. While Bonney and Moresby watched the valley we continued our advance until we were a few paces behind them.

Suddenly one of the horses whinnied. Moresby, who was nearest to the animals, turned his head in surprise.

'Drop them weapons, fellas,' Ben said.

Bonney wheeled around and started to bring up his rifle. I triggered the Henry and the round caught his thumb; he recoiled in pain as the Winchester sprang from his hands.

'You lowdown bastard!' he screamed.

Moresby looked into the barrels of our rifles and realized it would be a mistake to follow Bonney's lead; he gave us a surly look but threw down his weapon. Ben took their weapons and threw them over the ledge, then indicated the brush where the horses were tethered.

'I want you two to lead your horses up the hill,' he said. 'Wes and I will be right behind. Make any move we don't sanction and you'll breathe your last.'

Bonney took his bandanna and wrapped it around his hand, then he and Moresby took their horses' reins and began leading them up the trail. I untethered Toby's horse and, with Ben, followed them.

'How'd you find us?' Moresby asked, glancing back.

'Wasn't that difficult,' Ben replied. Bonney turned his head.

'That little shit Toby told you where we were, didn't he?' he said. 'I knew it was a mistake for him to watch the other side.'

'Both of you keep your eyes front and get a move on,' Ben replied.

Bonney and Moresby reached the rock where Toby was sitting just ahead of us. The man heard our approach and moved his head in an attempt to determine our position.

Bonney got to him first. He reached out and

yanked the gag from Toby's mouth.

'Is that you, Clay?' Toby asked. Ben waved the barrel of his Spencer at Bonney.

'Move away,' he said. 'Leave him be.'

'Yeah, it's us,' Clay Bonney answered Toby, ignoring Ben. 'You told these sons of bitches were we were at, didn't you, Toby?'

'Couldn't help it, Clay,' Toby said nervously. 'They got the drop on me.'

'Mean to tell me you couldn't've got off a warning shot?'

'Didn't have enough time, Clay.'

Bonney moved so quickly that there was no time to stop him. He lifted his foot and drove it hard into Toby's chest. The man was powerless to save himself: he pitched back from the rock and dropped head first into the ravine.

'You got an eternity now,' Bonney sneered. He watched Toby crash to the rocks below.

'That man was bound and blindfolded,' I said. 'He didn't have a chance.'

'Him givin' you our position gave us no chance,' answered Bonney.

Ben moved up and placed the barrel of his Spencer behind Bonney's ear.

'Another trick like that'll get you a bullet, mister,' he said. 'That's a promise.'

We made them lead their horses down the other side of the hill and carried on to where our mounts were tethered. Once there I covered Ben while he took a rope and bound Bonney's and Moresby's hands in front of them. We mounted up then and started back, with Bonney and Moresby leading. Ben and I brought up the rear with Toby's animal in tow.

Our captives remained silent until we reached the reached the shinnery oaks fork, where Ben directed the pair eastward and away from the main trail.

Bonney broke his silence.

'Ain't you swingin' a little wide, Turner?' He nodded to the main track. 'The trail to Copper Creek's over there.'

'We ain't going to Copper Creek,' Ben replied.

'Oh. Where're we headed?'

'Got you an appointment with some Mescalero Apaches.'

'You seen 'em?' Bonney sounded slightly panicked.

'They followed you to town.'

'And you volunteered to come and get us,' said Bonney. Moresby grunted.

'Can't believe you'd do the redskin's dirty work for 'em,' he said.

'It was either that or see the town attacked,' Ben told them. 'Which we're not about to let happen.'

'Ain't you aware the others'll have heard when your partner shot me?' asked Bonney.

'Given that some thought, yeah.'

'You got a reckoning comin', Turner. You'll pay for what happened to Clem. Lenny, too.'

'Could be your reckoning'll come first,' Ben replied.

CHAPTER FIFTEEN

The side trail a mile south-east of Copper Creek wound its way through high bedrock, where the sandstone split to form a narrow canyon. Here we rode in single file, with Bonney in front followed by Ben, Moresby and me. At the end of the cut was a sandstone pillar, where the trail forked left into a hollow dotted with boulders.

We cleared the cut and Ben reined his bay level with Bonney. I followed suit, moving my mare alongside Moresby.

Suddenly there was a staccato roar and a bullet ricocheted from a rock to our left. The sound of the shot echoed through the hollow, then someone called out.

'A little warning, *señores*,' a voice said. 'The next bullets will find your heads.'

Thirty feet ahead, behind a line of boulders standing at right angles to the trail, two men had their rifles aimed at Ben and me. They were bearded, heavyset and wore bandoleers across their chests.

'Chico!' Bonney exclaimed, 'Vicente! Ain't you two a sight for sore eyes.'

'*Muy bien*, Señor Bonney,' replied the man on the left. 'We heard a shot and went to the hill behind. Found tracks, realized you'd been taken.'

Bonney turned to Ben and grinned.

'Situation's changed some, ain't it, Turner?' He dug his heels into his animal's flanks and moved his horse in the Mexicans' direction. 'You find our guns, Chico?'

'*Sí*, Señor Bonney,' said the man on the left. 'Near the flat rock.'

Bonney's horse was now only a foot from Chico.

'Good,' he said. 'Cover these two till I get to you. I want to take care of them myself.'

I glanced at the Mexican called Vicente. His rifle was still trained on me, just as Chico's was on Ben. I looked at Moresby and saw him dig his heels into his horse's flanks with the intention of following Bonney. His mount walked just a few feet, however, then stopped. Moresby kicked the animal again, harder.

134

'Git up, damn you,' he said.

His horse whinnied in pain, then reared up and threw him.

The Mexicans' line of sight was temporarily obscured by the terrified horse and its falling rider. Ben and I took advantage and dismounted, then sprinted to a flat upright boulder.

Bonney had now reached the Mexican called Chico, who quickly freed him and returned his weapons. Moresby got his wind back and rolled behind the closest rock, ten feet short of Vicente.

The boulder where we were sheltering had deep notches at chest height, which allowed us to see Bonney and the Mexicans without exposing us from their position. Ben nodded towards Moresby.

'I'm going to try to get Bonney's sidekick to run. He's got less cover and is most likely to try to get to the others.'

'You gonna shoot him?'

'No, his hands are tied and he ain't armed. But we can target any shooter who gives him covering fire. Will you sight your rifle on the Mexes while I concentrate on Moresby?'

I saw Vicente rise clear of the rock, trigger his rifle, then duck down again. I noticed that with every other shot, however, he inched out and was more exposed.

Moresby soon became unsettled by Ben's fire. He rolled clear of the rock, rose to his feet, then ran to the Mexican's position. As Vicente moved out to give Moresby cover, I triggered the Henry. The Mexican slammed backwards as if he'd been hit with a pile-driver.

'One less, Wes,' said Ben. 'I see your aim's every bit as deadly as ever.'

' 'Cept now Moresby's reached cover,' I replied. 'We've still three guns to contend with.'

'I know, Wes. I couldn't shoot him tied and unarmed.'

'Nor could I, Ben. But we're still in a fix. If we don't get Bonney and Moresby, Copper Creek's in danger.'

Ben reloaded his rifle.

'You're right. I reckon there's still a couple of hours till sundown. Nothing for it but to keep trying. Your shot proves their position ain't that secure. They've got to raise up their heads every now and then to get off a shot.'

Bonney and Moresby were now behind an outcrop to the right, which abutted the hills we'd just passed through. They presented less of a target, however, as they didn't fire as often as Chico.

The Mexican employed a tactic of darting about. He shot at me over a boulder on the left, then went to the one on the right, where he targeted Ben. In between shots I caught a glimpse of him as he flitted across the gap. The space was only a couple of inches, but I figured if I timed my shot I'd a good chance of hitting him.

'That Mex is all over the place,' said Ben. 'Moresby and Bonney are getting off one shot to his two.'

'I know. I'm keeping an eye on him. He keeps moving between two rocks. There's a gap. I got my aim on it.'

'OK, Wes. Go for it. I'll keep the other two busy.'

I sighted the opening, but the Mexican moved so quickly that my first shot missed. The next time I counted the seconds until he drew level with the gap.

I got to four. Moments later he passed the opening and fired on Ben's position again.

I held my breath and concentrated: one . . . two . . . three . . . four.

Chico's body was a blur as I sent a bullet into the gap. This time I got a direct hit: blood spurted from the other side of the rock as the round found his chest. Ben glanced over as the Mexican went down.

'Good shot.'

'Thanks, Ben. Bit of luck to it, though.'

'Yeah. Wes, I've noticed that the oftener you

shoot, the luckier you get.' Ben gave a wry grin.

Bonney and Moresby, it seemed, had slowed their fire. I nodded towards the boulders where we'd last seen them.

'The other two ain't shooting,' I said. 'D'you reckon they're short on ammo?'

'Tell the truth, I dunno. There's been that much ordnance coming from the Mexican lately.'

Ben had his Spencer in a groove, sighted on Bonney and Moresby's last position. I placed my rifle in a niche at my end and aimed it in the same direction.

We studied the rocky outcrop for a while, but saw nothing.

'Helluva quiet,' Ben said. 'Nary a movement.'

Just then I heard a scuffle and felt the hairs prickling at the back of my neck.

'I'll be obliged if neither of you moved those rifles.' The voice was Bonney's.

Ben and I froze. I moved my head a fraction and saw him and Moresby standing on the rim behind us. Both had their rifles aimed and their fingers tight on the triggers.

'Drop your rifles and turn with your hands in the air,' Bonney ordered.

I gave Ben a sidelong glance. He remained impassive.

'I said drop those repeaters and turn with your hands up.' Bonney's voice rose.

Neither of us moved.

'We could always back-shoot you,' Bonney said. 'It'd give more satisfaction, though, to see the whites o' your eyes.'

'Yeah, turn around,' Moresby chimed in. 'I'm gonna get a kick outta this.'

Ben and I continued to look towards the outcrop.

'You must've circled around while your pal was taking the heat, huh, Bonney?' said Ben. 'Climbed up there and got the drop on us. Sly move.'

'I'm done talking, Turner,' Bonney said. 'You do as I say, or we shoot you in the back.'

Ben lowered his voice to a whisper.

'I'm gonna drop my rifle and turn fast. I'll try to pistol-shoot Bonney. You go for Moresby. Move when I throw my Spencer.'

'OK,' I replied. Ben glanced backwards.

'Looks like you're getting your reckoning after all, Bonney,' he said.

The next moments passed so fast it was as if time had speeded up.

Ben ditched his rifle and executed a lightning-fast turn. His hand went to his Colt. I turned a fraction later and reached for mine. Both of us were bringing our pistols to bear when we heard two rifle shots, one after the other.

I thought Bonney and Moresby had triggered their rifles, but when I looked up to the rim I saw Bonney stagger and drop his weapon. Then Moresby dropped to his knees, rolled along the ridge, and fell to the ground just a few paces from us.

Seconds later Bonney followed in a headlong dive and struck the canyon floor beside Moresby.

Ben looked as surprised as I was.

'Jeesus! I thought we were goners for a minute. The shots came from the other side of the rocks.'

'Yeah,' I replied, 'but who fired?'

CHAPTER SIXTEEN

I didn't have long to wait for an answer. We heard riders, then I saw Lone Wolf, Grey Owl and the other Apaches ride into the hollow from the north end.

Lone Wolf brought his pony to a standstill beside Bonney and Moresby, then dismounted and examined the bodies. Moments later he gave a grunt of satisfaction and spoke to two braves, who went over and took out their knives.

Each brave placed his knees on the shoulders of a dead man, made an incision around the scalp from forehead to the back of the neck, then pulled the scalp off by the hair. The braves took the scalps to Lone Wolf, who tucked them in a bag tied to his pony.

The Apache leader remounted, and then spoke

to Grey Owl.

'He say when you leave us outside town he think again about what you say,' said Grey Owl. 'He think you may tell the truth about these two being with the man called Holden. He send three warriors to follow you. The braves see you capture these men, trail you back from Holden's ranch. They also see the Mexicanos follow, think you may be in danger. They come back and report to Lone Wolf, then we come here.'

'Tell Lone Wolf thanks,' Ben said. 'He arrived in the nick of time. These men had their rifles trained on us. Wes and I mightn't have managed to overcome them.'

Again there was an exchange between Grey Owl and Lone Wolf.

'He say you brave men to risk your lives and he is grateful.'

Ben and I nodded and Lone Wolf spoke again.

'Lone Wolf say his warriors tell him Holden has many horses,' said Grey Owl.

'Yeah, that's true,' said Ben. 'At least fifty head.'

'They are his, or he steal them?'

'He's made a living by stealing. No reason to think he got his horses by any other means.'

Grey Owl translated for Lone Wolf, who clearly asked another question.

'He ask if you have objection to us taking his horses. Lone Wolf say it would punish Holden for giving these men shelter.'

'Tell Lone Wolf we'd be happy for him to take the horses,' replied Ben, 'but remind him that Holden still has a man with him. They'll be watching for an approach.'

On hearing this Lone Wolf pointed to the corpses of Bonney and Moresby and spoke again.

'Lone Wolf say if they give trouble they share the fate of these men,' said Grey Owl. Ben nodded.

'Tell Lone Wolf we wish you good luck.'

Lone Wolf put his arm across his chest, then waved it in salute and spoke again.

'He say: "go in peace",' said Grey Owl.

The sun was setting when we got back to Copper Creek. Mason and the other townsfolk met us and we brought them up to date. Mason confirmed that he'd seen us ride south.

'I'd an idea you were heading for Holden's place,' he said. 'When I saw that the Apaches were keeping their distance I thought you might have agreed something.'

'Glad it's over and you're back in one piece, anyhow,' said Sweet.

'You've done a marvellous job, boys,' Liam added.

'Amen to that,' said Billy Task.

Arthur Grace made his way to the front of the throng, with Eliza following.

'I'd like to add my vote of thanks,' he said. 'Copper Creek owes the two of you an enormous debt.'

Eliza pressed forward and took Ben's hand.

'I'm glad you're safe,' she said. 'I was so worried.'

I felt a tug at my sleeve. I turned and saw Abby.

'I'm glad, too, Wes,' she said, then she lowered her voice. 'Will you call in and see me, please? There's something I'd like to tell you.'

I arrived at Abby's house a short while later.

'I apologize, Wes,' she said when she opened the door. 'I meant to speak to you this morning, but Holden attacked the town and I couldn't. Billy Task came round and warned women and children to stay indoors.'

'Yeah, I'm sorry, too, Abby. I didn't have a chance to tell you myself. Ben and I were busy organizing the volunteers.'

'I understand.'

She went to Tommy's room and looked inside.

'It's OK, he's sleeping,' she said, then indicated a chair. 'Please, Wes, sit down. I wanted to talk about Luke . . . and us.'

144

'Is everything OK with you and Luke?'

'That's what I wanted to talk about.' She took my hand. 'After you left me last night I did a great deal of soul-searching. Wes, I was so stupid. After you'd gone I realized how much I loved you. I'm truly sorry if my indecision caused you pain. I was naive to imagine that Tommy's interests would be served by me taking Luke back.'

'You don't know how happy it makes me to hear you say that,' I said, then I remembered my conversation with Doherty the night before. 'Does Luke know?'

'Yes, I got Dora to keep an eye on Tommy for a little while and I went to his boarding house. It was quite late, but I told him it was over between us.'

'How did he take it?'

'He didn't say much. But he seemed to accept it. He told me he'd leave for El Paso this morning.'

'Do you know if he did?'

'Yes. Dora told me her husband saw him ride out before dawn.'

I leaned forward and kissed her.

'Then we can start over, Abby? I love you. You know that, don't you?'

'Of course, Wes,' she replied. 'You'll forgive me, darling, for hurting you?'

'There's nothing to forgive, Abby,' I said.

I took my leave a little later but I had arranged to see her the following night. We thought we'd have a meal at Mason's, then take in his new stereopticon show, which was featuring the Egyptian pyramids.

The next morning, however, Abby came into the store just before lunch. She looked distraught, and was dabbing her eyes with a handkerchief. I put down the box I was carrying and went to her side.

'What's the matter, Abby?'

'It's Tommy. Miss Lane just came by – she always brings Tommy home when school's out – she told me Tommy went to the gate to wait while she locked up. She heard a rider and turned and saw a man at the gate. Tommy went over and the rider swung him on to his saddle and rode off. I asked Miss Lane what the man looked like' – Abby paused and began sobbing – 'It was Luke, Wes. He's come back . . . he's abducted my son.'

'How long ago was this?'

'About forty minutes.'

'Did Miss Lane see which way they went?'

'She said they were heading south.'

While we were talking Ben came through from the storeroom and Eliza left the counter and hurried over. She put her arm around Abby's shoulders.

'Don't worry, Abby. Wes and Ben will ride after

him. It shouldn't be long till they catch up.'

'I'm so frightened he'll hurt Tommy,' wailed Abby.

'I shouldn't worry about that, Abby. He wouldn't hurt his own son,' said Eliza.

Ben and I saddled up and rode out at a fast gallop. In the preceding twenty-four hours there'd been neither wind nor rain, and Doherty's tracks were still clearly visible on the trail south of town.

We quickly covered the same ground as we had the day before, and soon came to the fork leading to Holden's ranch. The tracks continued past the cottonwoods, however, and from there the trail wound through some low hills for another three miles. There the road took a dogleg through a thick patch of mesquite, and a hundred yards further on we came to a glade where an appaloosa was tethered.

Ben and I dismounted and went to the animal. Then we saw footprints at the edge of the glade. While I pulled up the saddle and examined the horse's withers Ben took a closer look at the tracks.

'This animal's worked up a fair lather, Ben,' I said. 'It ain't been roped long. It's gotta be Doherty's.'

Ben pointed to the footprints.

'Yeah, somebody's been here. One set of boot-marks. Fresh and fairly deep. Likely made by someone carrying the weight of a boy. They go up the side of the glade.'

'But why leave his horse here?' I asked.

'Can't say,' Ben replied. 'If either he or the boy needed to relieve themselves they wouldn't need to go far off the trail. Nothing else for it but for us to follow the tracks. See where they lead.'

Ben and I tethered our mounts and walked into the glade, which was encircled by large cedars and curved to the right a short way along. Ben and I held close to the bordering cedars and made our way around the curve.

We cleared the corner and looked to the top of the glade. Doherty and Tommy stood facing us with their backs to the trees.

'What's the hell's going on?' I whispered.

'Don't know,' Ben replied. 'Doherty's just stand-ing there with the boy. He doesn't appear to be armed.'

As if in answer, a voice called out:

'Why don't you and your sidekick come out where we can see you, Turner? Don't want to have to shoot the boy.'

CHAPTER SEVENTEEN

I looked beyond where Doherty stood, and saw Holden and Dunstan standing at the edge of the trees. Both had rifles aimed at Tommy and his father. Then Doherty spoke.

'I'm sorry, Noble,' he said tensely. 'I was angry at Abby for rejecting me and that's why I took Tommy. I was going to take him to El Paso. Thought better of it a mile south of town. Was in the act of bringing him back when these two waylaid me. Found out we were headed to Copper Creek and held me at gunpoint, forced us up here. The boy mentioned your name and Holden cottoned on. Got me to admit what I'd done. He made me tether my roan at the start of the draw and leave footprints. He guessed you'd see them and follow me.'

'That's right,' Holden said. 'Wasn't mistaken, was I? You sold me out to those redskins, didn't you, Turner? Forced me to leave or else face a scalping. Thieving bastards took my horses and left me with nothing. Now I'm getting even.' He waved the barrel of his rifle at Doherty and Tommy. 'Throw down your guns and step out where we can see you. Do it now, else these two'll get shot.'

While Holden spoke Ben and I continued to edge our way up. Using the trees as cover, we had come within only a dozen paces from Doherty and Tommy.

'Don't come any nearer, Turner,' Holden said. 'Throw down your weapons and come out from those trees. I'll shoot the boy if you don't. Won't tell you again.'

'Why don't you let Tommy and his father go, Holden?' Ben said. 'This fight's just between us. You and Dunstan come out. We'll settle it face to face.'

Holden gave a sarcastic laugh.

'That'd suit you better, wouldn't it, Turner? No, I ain't that much of a fool . . . or that much of a gambler.'

Suddenly Doherty took action: he hooked his

hands under Tommy's arms and lifted the boy clear of the ground. Holding Tommy close to shield him, he began running in our direction.

Holden reacted quickly and began firing. Almost immediately Doherty was hit in the back. He staggered, but continued to shield Tommy as he struggled to close the gap between us.

As Doherty legs weakened and he fell to his knees, Ben dived from the trees and rolled into the glade. He raised himself on to his elbows and sighted his Spencer, then he returned fire to take the heat off Doherty. Then another bullet hit Doherty. He pushed his son forward.

'Run to Wes, Tommy,' he said, gasping for breath. 'Hurry. Run as fast as you ca . . .' His voice trailed off and he slumped to the ground.

I darted out and grabbed Tommy. I had only just managed to pull him to shelter when shots splintered the timber around us.

Ben, meanwhile, had found a slight rise in the glade and continued to fire. Now that Tommy no longer presented a target Holden joined his sidekick and began shooting at Ben.

I took the boy a few feet into the timber, out of harm's way.

'Stay here, Tommy,' I said. 'Everything's gonna be all right. Don't move, OK?'

'OK, Wes.'

I went back to the edge of the trees and shouldered my Henry. Ben was still pinned down by both shooters. Dunstan was the closer, exposed only when he fired from the side of a pine tree, rather than the fork of a low branch which was his favoured vantage point. I waited until he moved to the side, then fired; the bullet caught him high in the chest and he fell back.

When he saw that Dunstan had been hit Holden backed into the trees. Seconds later I heard the sound of hoofbeats, then a big roan cleared the trees and rode towards Ben at a fast gallop.

Holden had the animal's reins between his teeth and two .45s in his hands. The height of his mount compromised Ben's cover as Holden blasted his position.

I brought up my Henry, but the roan was a blur and I'd no time for a telling shot. I could only watch in trepidation as Holden's bullets kicked the earth around Ben and the horse bore down on his position.

Ben spun right, however, away of the threshing hoofs and spitting bullets. As the roan drew level, he brought up his Spencer and fired: the round caught Holden's forehead and his back arched. The forward movement of the roan spun Holden clear of the saddle; he somersaulted over the animal's hindquarters and hit the ground hard.

Ben got up and walked over to Doherty, then turned him over and put an ear to his chest. He raised his head.

' 'Fraid he's gone, Wes,' he said.

'I'll get Tommy,' I replied, 'and we'll skirt the trees to the end of the draw.' I nodded towards Doherty and the other two. 'No need for him to see this.'

'Yeah,' Ben agreed. 'We'll leave the bodies here for now. Gorman's picking up the corpses of Bonney and the others north of Holden's place this afternoon. I'll ask him to add these to his tally when we get back.'

I went to where Tommy was and took him into my arms, then walked to the end of the draw. Halfway there he gave me an earnest look.

'Have the bad men gone away, Wes?' he asked. I hugged him close and tousled his hair.

'Yes, Tommy, they've all gone.'

Abby was waiting at the gate when we got back. As soon as she saw Tommy she threw her hands to her face in an expression of relief.

'Oh, Tommy, darling,' she said. 'Thank God you're safe!' I lifted Tommy from the saddle and she took him in her arms. We went inside and she gave him a glass of milk. Soon after the boy had drunk it his eyes began to close.

'He's sleepy,' Abby said. 'I'll put him to bed for a while.'

When she came back I explained what had happened.

'So Luke sacrificed his life to save Tommy's?'

'Yes,' I replied. 'It was wrong of him to take the boy, but what he did proved his love for his son.'

She took a handkerchief and dabbed her eyes.

'You're right. And I'll always be grateful to him for that. But I've you and Ben to thank for rescuing Tommy, and for ending Holden's reign of terror.' She put her arms around my waist then and kissed me. 'And I'd like to tell you again how much I love you.'

I pulled her closer.

'I love you, too, Abby. You'll take me up on my offer, then?'

'To marry you, you mean?'

'Yes.'

'Of course, Wes, darling. Of course.'

The following Thursday Eliza was tending the counter and Ben and I were in the storeroom taking a break. We were drinking coffee and ruminating on recent events.

'Amazing to think of the change that can be wrought in a man's life in just a few weeks,' Ben said.

'Yeah,' I agreed. 'This time last month we were still pannin' the Canadian. Who'da thought it? Since then we've helped to tame a town and got us a business. Both of us'll be hitched, too, 'fore long.'

'Did I tell you Eliza's asked to stay on?'

I swallowed some coffee and put down the cup.

'Yeah, you did. Eliza's also asked Abby if she'd like to run her dressmaking business from the store. Easier than working from home.'

'Yeah, good idea,' Ben said. 'Two them get along just fine.'

'Help Abby, too. Be good company for each other.'

'Of course,' Ben said. 'How's Tommy by the way?'

'Back to normal now. Easier for kids that age to put bad things behind them.'

'Yeah, reckon it is.'

Eliza came through to the storeroom at that moment and smiled at us.

'You boys finished your coffee?'

'Yeah, we have, Eliza,' Ben replied. 'You want to see to your father's lunch?'

'Yes, please, Ben,' she replied, then added, 'Oh,

I nearly forgot. There's a drummer out front from a tailoring supplier in Silver City. Comes in every couple of months looking for an order. Bit on the expensive side, so Father's always passed. You might want to see him, though. If you'd like to add suits to our range.'

'OK, Eliza,' Ben said, 'we'll have a word with him. Did the man give his name?'

Eliza put on her hat and went to the back door.

'Bannister,' she replied. 'Grover Bannister.'

Ben and I went through to the front. Bannister looked much as he had when we saw him weeks earlier: the same heavy woollen suit and high-collar shirt. He had his derby hat in one hand and used a kerchief to mop his brow with the other. He turned as we walked through the door and did a double take.

'You're the fellas I met at Twin Buttes,' he said in surprise. 'You're working for Mr Grace now?'

'No sir, we ain't,' Ben replied.

'Then how. . . ?'

'Mr Grace has retired,' I said. 'We bought the store from him three weeks ago.'

Bannister shook his kerchief and put it back in his pocket.

'Oh, I see. I didn't think ...' He checked himself and left the sentence hanging.

'Didn't think we had the wherewithal to become storekeepers?' Ben gave a thin smile.

'Yes – no – I mean . . .' Bannister looked flustered.

'It's OK,' Ben said. 'We're still getting used to the idea ourselves.'

'Ah, well, yes,' Bannister regained his composure, 'I guess it's different from prospecting.'

'So, what can we do for you?'

Bannister lifted a large leather case on to the counter, undid the straps, and opened the top.

'I was wondering if you gentlemen might consider stocking our latest line in men's suits.' He took out a pair of suit pants and draped them across the counter.

'These are the pants,' he said. 'Like the coat, made from the finest worsted fabric. Very durable, but also very light; ideal for the Texas climate.' He took one of the pant legs and played the cloth between his thumb and forefinger. 'Here, feel the texture.'

Ben felt the cloth.

'Yeah, good quality. How much?'

'Well, the complete suits come in a variety of sizes, ready made. Ten dollars retail. Your price is only fifty-five dollars a dozen, of course.'

'Too expensive for our customers, I'm afraid,'

Ben told him.

'Really? I thought you'd have a lot of miners passing through. Drovers, too. Men in those jobs are quite well paid, aren't they? Likely to appreciate fancy duds for their payday perambulations.'

'No, I don't think so, Bannister, sorry.'

'Oh, well.' Bannister accepted defeat. 'Anyway, I'm glad we meet under more auspicious circumstances than on the last occasion.'

'Ah yes, Lone Wolf and his braves,' I joined in. 'Nothing more to fear there, Mr Bannister. There was the threat of an attack on Sunday, but they've moved on now.'

'The . . . the Apaches were here?' Bannister went white.

'Yeah, Lone Wolf and sixty braves were just outside Copper Creek four days ago,' I said. 'Almost attacked the town.'

'W-which way did they go?' Panic rose in his voice.

'Back to Twin Buttes, I think.'

Bannister grabbed the suit pants and stuffed them back into the case.

'Oh, my God! I was heading that way.' He hurriedly strapped the case and headed out of the store.

'Yeah,' I said, 'but there's no—'

158

'No need to be concerned?' Bannister interrupted. 'The hell you say!' His hands were trembling as he fumbled for the door handle. 'Came damn near a scalping the last time I ran into those savages. Don't want to risk it ever again.'

Ben and I went out on to the boardwalk and watched as Bannister grabbed his horse's reins and mounted hurriedly. He took the rope of his burro.

'They'll not be satisfied till they've scalped half the county in revenge for their kin,' he shouted. 'You mark my words.'

He spurred his horse and set off, riding south at a fast gallop. His burro kicked as the rope tautened; then it followed, heehawing its protests and leaving a cloud of dust in its wake.

'But Bannister,' I called after him, 'the Apaches found the men who did it, they . . .'

'No use, Wes,' said Ben. 'He can't hear you.'

'I don't know what got him so all fired up. I was trying to explain the danger was over.'

'Didn't want to stick around, I suppose. The very mention of Apaches seemed to loosen his bowels.'

I smiled. 'Ah . . . well, at least he's got a spare pair of pants with him.'

Ben's belly shook and he began to convulse with mirth.

'Just hope they're his size.'

Seconds later the two of us were rolling on the boardwalk, hugging our sides and roaring with laughter.